Animal Magic

Have you read them all?

Look out for more books by
HOLLY WEBB

EMILY
FEATHER
and the Enchanted Door

www.holly-webb.com

Animal Magic

Hamstermagic

SCHOLASTIC

HOLLY WEBB

Scholastic Children's Books
An imprint of Scholastic Ltd
Euston House, 24 Eversholt Street
London, NW1 1DB, UK
Registered office: Westfield Road, Southam, Warwickshire, CV47 0RA
SCHOLASTIC and associated logos are trademarks and/or
registered trademarks of Scholastic Inc.

First published in the UK by Scholastic Ltd, 2009
This edition published by Scholastic Ltd, 2013

ISBN 978 1 407 13554 0

A CIP catalogue record for this book is available
from the British Library.

Printed and bound by CPI Group (UK) Ltd, Croydon, CR0 4YY
Papers used by Scholastic Children's Books are made from
wood grown in sustainable forests.

5 7 9 10 8 6 4

www.scholastic.co.uk/zone

For Jon, Tom, Robin and William

Chapter 1

"I am glad I do not have to go out," Sofie said smugly, peering out at the dark street. She gave a luxurious little shiver, setting her big dachshund ears quivering, and yawned. "Put on your scarf, Lottie. Fog is very bad for the chest." She settled herself more comfortably on her purple velvet cushion, wrapping her smooth, black tail tightly round her bottom as though she was afraid of draughts. She looked very much an indoor dog, Lottie thought enviously, with her polished black coat and delicate ginger eyebrows.

Lottie looked out of the window at the misty swirls wreathing the lamp post, and shivered. It was only the third week of October, but autumn had turned up with a vengeance. She picked up her school bag and winced – she was sure it felt lighter when the weather was sunny. "Bye, Uncle Jack!" she called through to the kitchen at the back of the shop.

Her uncle wandered out to wave goodbye, crunching a piece of toast, and Lottie gave him a rather resentful look. He still had his slippers on. It just wasn't fair. Still, she had to go. She was supposed to be meeting Ruby halfway to school.

"Come home quickly after school, Lottie," Uncle Jack reminded her thickly through a mouthful of peanut butter. "Interesting new delivery coming today, from that supplier down on the coast. New mice, I think!"

Lottie nodded, feeling a little more cheerful. She had been living at her uncle's pet shop for nearly three months, while her mother was abroad. Lottie's mum worked in Paris now, since her company had transferred her to their French office. It had been a huge upheaval for Lottie to leave all her friends, and stay with Uncle Jack and Danny for the holidays, and she'd been furious about it.

She'd been even more upset when her mum had told that it wouldn't be just a few weeks in Netherbridge as she'd expected. The French job had been extended, and Lottie would have to start the new school term in Netherbridge too. But she loved the shop now – so much so that she couldn't imagine going home again. The shop was full of the most amazing magical creatures, most of whom talked, and one of the best bits was that Uncle Jack kept finding new ones. New animals were always exciting, and the mice were some of the funniest creatures they had.

As she opened the shop door, she heard her favourite pink mice starting to argue about where the new mice's cage would go. "Next to us!" they were pleading with Uncle Jack. "Can't you move Septimus's cage? He's always at school with Danny anyway – we hardly ever see him."

Septimus was a black rat, who'd overcome his habitual laziness to accompany Lottie's cousin to school. Danny was in his first year at secondary school, and hated it. He'd been very lonely at first, but he was far too proud to admit it. Septimus, who adored him anyway, had volunteered to keep him company if sufficiently bribed with peanut brittle. Together they seemed to be plotting the overthrow of the National Curriculum, but at least Danny seemed a bit happier at school.

Grace's Pet Shop was in the middle of one of the main shopping streets in Netherbridge, but the whole town was old-fashioned, with narrow roads, and lots of cobbles, and pretty bridges over the river. At this end of the street, the black-and-white timbered houses leaned closer together over the road, the walls bulging, as though the houses were half alive. Lottie sniffed the air as she set off down the street. It was slightly sour, and smoky.

Netherbridge looked like something out of a television drama, the kind where everyone wore big frilly petticoats. She expected a coach and horses to gallop down the street beside her, the coachman yelling at his team of horses, hurrying them along to escape the highwaymen with their pistols. The coiling mist thickened, just like a stage effect, and Lottie listened for the thunder of hooves. Or maybe a vampire ought to glide out from one of those dark alleyways. She moved slightly further into the middle of the street.

Lottie shivered, and shook herself. Why was she letting the mist get to her like this? It was just weather, nothing spooky about it. Still, she caught her breath when figures started to approach her out of the greyish fog. Especially as one did seem to be wrapped in a long black cloak, just like bat wings. . .

"Nonsense! Absolute nonsense! A myth!" Lottie sighed out a shaky breath of relief. Vampires didn't talk like that. Probably, anyway. Lottie added vampires to her mental list of things to ask Uncle Jack about. Dragons had turned out to be real, after all, even though the pair she knew were only cat-sized.

The misty figures turned into two solid men, one tall, one extremely short, and both arguing.

"I tell you, I saw it! Charging about on Netherbridge Hill! Horn a foot long!" The little man was getting so cross that his face had turned scarlet, and the mist looked like steam billowing from his ears.

"Sssshhh!" His companion had noticed Lottie approaching, and obviously didn't want to be overheard.

"Stop fussing, you overgrown beanpole, it's only Grace's girl. Whatsername. Lily." The short one peered through the fog at Lottie. "Lara? Lucy?"

"Lottie," said Lottie, giggling.

"Lottie. Exactly. Like I said. Did you know there was a unicorn up on Netherbridge Hill, Louisa?"

Lottie shook her head, not sure whether to believe him or not. She recognized him now – Mr Fieldfare, who came to the shop sometimes to buy bird seed. He lived up north somewhere, but Grace's was one of the few magic pet shops in the country, so many of the customers travelled a long way for their supplies. Mr Fieldfare had a flock of brilliantly coloured finches flying free in his house, Uncle Jack said. Mr Fieldfare didn't call them finches, though – he always spoke of them as his feathered jewels.

"This is Jacob, Laura, my old friend Jacob Bucklebank. Staying with me for Halloween, you see. Had to come down here to the shop to get some special treats for my darlings, for the celebration."

Mr Bucklebank bowed very low, sweeping off his big black hat. He had flowing dark hair, and a dark, silky beard. Mr Fieldfare was what Uncle Jack called a financial wizard, which – as far as Lottie understood it – was a mixture of being good with money and a little extra magical something. But he didn't *look* very magical. Lottie found it hard to imagine magicians being short and fat. By contrast, his friend gave off an air of spells bubbling at his fingertips.

They waved to her, continuing their friendly squabble as they strolled on through the mist, and left Lottie wondering.

Halloween.

She'd only been living at the shop since July, the beginning of the summer holidays, but it hadn't taken her more than a couple of weeks to realize that it wasn't an ordinary shop. People came to it from all over the country. They came to buy Uncle Jack's amazing home-made remedies (a better word to put on the labels than *spells*) and to ask him about their problems with bad-tempered tortoises, and cats who couldn't spell. There were a lot of local customers, too. But most of them had no idea what was really in the cages that looked empty. They never saw the pink mice, or Horace the parrot doing the crossword. They didn't know about the magic.

What would Halloween be like now that she knew magic was real? The toy shop had a window full of witch's hats and plastic monster masks, and everyone at school was talking about trick or treating, just like they would be back at her old school. But Lottie couldn't help feeling that after all the children had gone to bed, feeling sick from too many sweets, Halloween would be *real* . . . and rather scary. What did Uncle Jack do on Halloween? What about Ariadne, his girlfriend, who was teaching Lottie magic? Was there some strange ritual they all went off to take part in at midnight? Lottie shivered at the thought.

"Lottie!" Ruby was waving to her from the bridge. "Come on, we're going to be late!"

Lottie checked her watch — Ruby was right, she must have slowed up in the mist more than she'd realized. "Sorry!" she called, running over. The mist was thinner on the bridge. Ruby's red hair gleamed through it, and she looked reassuringly normal and not at all spooky.

"Horrible weather, isn't it?" she said cheerfully as they set off along River Street. "Just right for school. I really hate Mondays. Having PE on a Monday morning is just cruel."

They joined the stream of children heading for the school gates, and Lottie couldn't talk to Ruby about what she'd been thinking, for fear of being overheard. Ruby had no magical powers herself, but she was a good friend and Lottie had told her the truth about what the pet shop really was. Ruby had also seen her and Sofie working magic – as Lottie's familiar, Sofie strengthened her powers and their minds were linked too. Although Ruby couldn't do that sort of thing, she'd helped Lottie with a spell here at school only a couple of weeks ago, and Lottie liked that there was at least one "normal" person in her life that she could talk to about homework and TV, instead of herbs, and how to stop mice misbehaving.

Lottie and Ruby headed for one of the benches up against the wall of the school, hoping for some shelter. "I need to find some gloves," Lottie muttered. "Mum sent a parcel of clothes for me from France, and they're gorgeous, but I wish I had all my old things too. Loads of my winter stuff is packed away in storage, now that she's rented out our old flat." She sighed, thinking of her favourite pink fluffy gloves lying at the bottom of a box somewhere.

"Is she coming back over any time soon?" Ruby asked.

Lottie shook her head. "They're real slave-drivers. She even has to work over the weekends a lot of the time. But she thinks she might be able to pop over on the Eurostar for a weekend, in a few weeks' time."

Ruby nodded sympathetically. Her mother was an artist, and even though she worked in her studio at the bottom of the garden, sometimes she might as well be on the other side of the world. Ruby was quite used to getting her own tea. But at least she could see her mum whenever she wanted.

"Ah well," Ruby said, fluttering her eyelashes. "If your mum hadn't had to go to Paris, you'd never have met *me*."

Lottie rolled her eyes, and swatted Ruby with her literacy homework. She'd been too busy helping Uncle Jack make a batch of his special sugar mice to do it last night. Actually, she just hated writing poems, because hers always sounded stupid. It didn't make any difference how long she spent doing it.

"Oh my word," Ruby muttered, staring across the playground. "What is Zara Martin wearing?"

Zara and her little clique had just strolled into the playground, ignoring everyone else.

"She looks like she's got a stuffed cat on her head," Lottie giggled. Then she gave Ruby a horrified look. "You don't think that's real fur, do you?"

Ruby looked thoughtfully at Zara, now modelling her new fur hat for the rest of the girls in their class. "No," she said at last. "Zara wouldn't put a dead animal on her head. Last year when we were in Year Five she wouldn't even touch our class hamster. She hates animals."

Lottie nodded disgustedly. She'd met Zara a couple of times in the school holidays, and hated her before she'd even found out they were in the same class. She and Sofie had actually rescued a skinny little stray cat from Zara and her gang (though Sofie now refused to admit any part in this – she was not a cat fan), which had only made Zara more of an enemy. Lottie had taken the cat back to the shop, half reluctantly. She hadn't been sure what Uncle Jack would say about letting a starved little stray who couldn't talk live with his clever magical animals. But Tabitha had turned out to have magical powers of her own, and Lottie had found her a wonderful home with

Ariadne, as her new familiar.

"Are you doing anything for Halloween?" she asked Ruby quietly, remembering her earlier thoughts.

"No. My mum really hates all that Halloween stuff. She makes us all sit in the living room with the curtains drawn and pretend we're out. I mean, she'd probably let me go to a Halloween party, but she hates trick or treating. She says it's all just made up to sell things. Why, anyway? Do you want to go?"

"No. . ." Lottie wasn't quite sure what to say. She didn't want to sound stupid. "I went trick or treating last year with friends from my old school. I don't mind not doing it again. It's just that I couldn't help feeling, this morning, that Halloween might be a bit, well, *dangerous*. . ."

Ruby looked at her as if she was dippy. "What – are you worried someone might give you a nasty nip with their plastic vampire teeth?" she asked, grinning.

Lottie stared at her fingers, and muttered quietly, "But what if it's not all plastic?"

"Oh!" Ruby's smile faded. "Oh, I see what you mean. . ."

"Everyone dresses up, and it's fun and silly and not really scary. But what if the things they're dressing up as are real?" Lottie shivered.

"I hadn't thought of it like that," Ruby admitted.

"Halloween's a special night for witches, isn't it?" Lottie asked. She didn't know much about the history of witchcraft. "It's more than just sweets and pumpkins. And we know witches really exist."

"Well, of course we do, you *are* one," Ruby pointed out.

Lottie shook her head firmly. "I'm only Ariadne's apprentice. I don't know what I'm doing with most magic yet. That settles it, I'm staying indoors and watching TV this Saturday. Even if I get invited to the best

Halloween party ever!"

The mist had cleared by the time they walked home from school, leaving a beautiful, crisp October day, but Lottie's unease still lingered. She *was* a witch. Ariadne had said so, after the spell Lottie had cast on Zara a couple of weeks ago. Zara had tried to set Lottie up, so it looked as though she'd cheated in a test, and Lottie had protected herself with a spell. Until then, she'd been too nervous to do a spell on her own. She was actually grateful to Zara, in a weird sort of way. And she wasn't scared of her any more. Lottie still hated her, but the spell had broken the hold Zara had over Lottie.

Ruby said that it was a great waste that everyone else in the class had forgotten it happening, but Lottie wasn't so sure. Zara didn't have the same power over the class as she'd had before. Her own little gang still followed her around like puppies, but some of the other girls had dared to stand up to her recently. It was as though Lottie's spell had broken the one that Zara had over them too.

Lottie blinked, and stopped still in the middle of the pavement. Ruby had gone on to her house, so luckily she was alone to think this out. *Zara's* spell? Lottie hadn't really meant that Zara was a witch too — but was there any reason why she shouldn't be? She'd certainly had some strange, almost unnatural hold over everyone else in Lottie's class.

Lottie walked on slowly. No. Zara couldn't be. Lottie would have felt it when she laid the spell on her. And Zara wouldn't have been so scared because she'd have known what Lottie was doing. Possibly Zara had some power, deep down, that she used for bullying and manipulating other people, without realizing what it was. But she wasn't really magical. Lottie breathed a shaky sigh of relief. The idea of Zara as a witch was just too scary. She was quite bad enough as she was. Magic had been fun for Lottie so far, most of the time. Zara would poison it, turn it to something dark and horrible. The kind of thing that had been preying on Lottie's mind that morning, for instance.

Lottie scowled as she pushed open the shop door. She didn't want to think about that kind of thing. She wasn't ready for the darker side of magic. Like she'd told Ruby, she was staying in on Halloween – with a big bar of chocolate.

Sofie ran across the shop to meet her, weaving in and out of her legs with pleasure. Usually she was a very dignified little dog, but she did occasionally let her smart manners lapse. Even though Sofie said she hated the idea of school, Lottie knew that really she hated that they had to be apart for most of the day. She and Lottie could read each other's minds, but it wasn't the same as being together.

Lottie picked Sofie up, and Sofie gave a huge yawn, suddenly remembering to be sophisticated. "School – nothing happened, as usual?" she asked, flapping a paw vaguely.

"Lottie! Perfect timing!" Uncle Jack sounded excited. He was standing by the counter, just starting to open a big cardboard pet carrier box. "It's just been delivered, the new mouse shipment. Very rare and interesting apparently."

"Not as rare as us?" one of the pink mice asked anxiously, climbing through his cage door and peering over from the edge of the shelf. "I'm ever so interesting," he added importantly, starting to scurry down the shelf towards the counter. "Even more than the others – they're asleep, which is really just boring, isn't it?"

"You're the most interesting mouse I know, Fred," Lottie told him reassuringly, stroking his soft rose-petal fur with one finger.

"Really?" he asked delightedly. "Even more than Henrietta?"

This was a tricky one, as Henrietta, the homing mouse, was quite remarkable. She didn't live in a group, like the pink mice or the shy, pink-eyed white ones. She was a lone operator. Uncle Jack sold her to people he thought didn't deserve pets, and then a few days later she came back, having thoroughly put her new owners off pet-keeping. Whenever Lottie had seen her, she'd been a very pretty cocoa-powder brown, like a little furry truffle, but she had a variety of disguises. "Henrietta is clever, but you have character," Lottie said solemnly.

"Oh!" Fred the mouse twirled his whiskers shyly, rather overcome. He skittered up Lottie's arm to perch on her shoulder, watching Uncle Jack unfasten the box.

Sofie jumped down, yawning again. "Mice, huh! Why such a fuss? Wake me if they really are interesting," she muttered from her cushion, turning round and tucking her nose more comfortably between her paws. Lottie could feel her in the back of her mind, already deep in a warm, soft, velvety doze.

Lottie stood on tiptoe to peer into the box as Uncle Jack lifted up the flaps, and Fred teetered on Lottie's shoulder as he leaned over to look too.

"Oh!" Uncle Jack frowned.

"That's not a mouse," Fred said, sounding rather disgusted. "I don't know *what* it is."

In a ball of crumpled paper bedding, a fat orange and white creature was curled up, fast asleep and snoring buzzily.

"There must have been a mix-up," Uncle Jack said disappointedly. "I definitely didn't order a hamster. I'll have to send it back."

"Can *we* see?" a silky voice purred from the edge of the counter, and Lottie jumped as Selina and Sarafan, the black cats, suddenly appeared on either side of the box, their whiskers twitching with excitement. Lottie was sure that Selina was drooling.

"How did you two get out?" Uncle Jack demanded, patting his pockets. "Sarafan, did you steal my keys again?" Uncle Jack didn't like shutting any of the animals up, but Selina and Sarafan couldn't be trusted around the mice. Now that they'd learned how to open latches, he was forced to padlock their enormous pen.

"If you don't want this furry thing. . ." Sarafan suggested meaningfully.

"We're ever so short of exercise," Selina agreed, poking her nose into the box, her whiskers brushing the orange fur. Lottie could see all of her teeth.

"Selina, no!" Uncle Jack snapped. "This isn't a cat toy." He tried to hold Selina and Sarafan away but they were even harder to keep a grip on than ordinary cats and seemed to flow around his fingers, ending up with their front paws on the edge of the box.

"It *looks* like one," Selina purred.

At this point, the gently snoring orange ball woke up.

Lottie had been expecting that a hamster's reaction to a cat only a nose-length away would be similar to a mouse's. Fred was currently cowering inside her cardigan. But the hamster opened its beady black eyes and blinked sleepily. Then the eyes sparkled, like little black diamonds, and he sat up. "Harrumph! Haven't been introduced. Most irregular. Very rude to invade a gentleman's privacy, particularly when asleep. An English hamster's bedding is his castle, and all that!"

Then he bit Selina on the nose.

Lottie couldn't help laughing. She'd never seen Selina move so fast. The two black cats were back in their pen in the far room in seconds, sulking in private.

The hamster looked up hopefully. "I don't suppose you would have any sunflower seeds to take the taste away, would you? Cat is so rancid, particularly that sort of under-bred feline."

There was a hissing gasp from the cats' pen and the hamster winked at Lottie.

Uncle Jack filled a small china bowl with sunflower seeds and put it on the counter. "Would you prefer to stay in the box, or may I lift you out?" he asked politely.

"Oh, out, please," the hamster replied. "Must inspect the new quarters, what?"

Uncle Jack put a hand into the box and the hamster waddled on to it. He was rather portly but it suited him, Lottie thought. He was a very dignified little creature. He stepped off on to the counter and looked approvingly at the bowl. "Very nice. Wedgewood?" he asked, running a paw over the pattern.

"Er, yes, I think so." Uncle Jack blinked. He didn't like boring brown food bowls and tended to buy little china bowls for the animals' seed mixes whenever he saw them in junk shops. But he'd never had an animal in the shop who could discuss china patterns. Lottie noticed that Uncle Jack seemed to have forgotten about sending the hamster back.

"Do excuse me," the hamster bowed apologetically. "Those little harridans have made me forget my manners. My name is Giles."

Lottie half curtseyed and Uncle Jack bowed his head politely. Giles had that effect. "I'm Jack Grace, owner of the shop, and this is my niece, Lottie. Er . . . how do you do? Was it a tiring journey?"

"Not at all, not at all," Giles replied through several sunflower seeds. He eyed Lottie interestedly, with his head on one side. "Lottie? So you'd be Lottie Grace then, would you? Mmm. I've heard of you."

Chapter 2

"Heard of me?" Lottie repeated, staring at Giles in confusion.

"Yes, and not in the most flattering terms, I'm afraid." Giles munched a sunflower seed, staring thoughtfully at her.

"But . . . I don't understand. . ." Lottie faltered.

"Well, your uncle bought me from an animal importers, you see. Horrible place, not at all the sort of animals I like to associate with. Low morals. A lot of cats."

Uncle Jack looked apologetic. "I hadn't used them before. I had heard they were rather good, but perhaps I won't order from them again."

"I wouldn't." Giles nodded approvingly. "The owner was a most unpleasant man and I did not like the clientele. I have to admit, I was somewhat worried about this shop. But you seem quite respectable after all."

Lottie and Uncle Jack exchanged a glance, half relieved, half amused. Neither of them wanted to be disapproved of by a hamster.

"So was it one of the customers who was talking about me?" Lottie asked curiously.

"Mmm. She bought two salukis. I think she'd had them specially brought from Egypt. Very valuable dogs – it was an important order." Giles shuddered. "Horrible things. So skinny, it was unnatural. And they had hungry eyes," he added darkly. "The woman who bought them – she must have been a friend of the owner. They talked for a long time. They didn't seem to care that I could hear them, but the sort of things they were saying – *ugh*." He looked up at Lottie. "She didn't like you at all, Lottie. I should do my best to avoid that one if I were you." He ate another sunflower seed for comfort. "Particularly if those dogs are with her."

Lottie nodded and looked worriedly at Uncle Jack. His face was oddly blank, as though he knew something she didn't and had no intention of telling her what. "You know who it is, don't you?" she asked him accusingly.

Uncle Jack shrugged. "I think so. I imagine it's the enchantress who came into the shop a few weeks ago." He sniffed disgustedly. "Enchantress? Murderess more like. . ."

"Did you *know* her?" Lottie stared at him. "You didn't say!"

"I'm not saying now." Uncle Jack folded his lips tightly and stared out of the window.

"Which means you do," Lottie observed and watched his eyebrows twitch with irritation. "Was she wearing a red dress, this woman who bought the salukis?" she asked Giles. "Long blonde hair, almost white?"

"That's the one," Giles mumbled with his mouth full. "Nasty piece of work. You stay out of her way, my dear."

Lottie nodded. She would do her best. But it was worrying to hear that someone like that had remembered her. Not only remembered her but had been talking about her, maybe even plotting against her. Lottie shivered. Uncle Jack was still looking unusually grim and he obviously didn't intend to discuss it.

"All I did was stop her bewitching me," she told him pleadingly. "I don't know why she hates me so much. . ."

Uncle Jack put his arm around her shoulders. "It's nothing to do with you, Lottie love. It all happened before you were born, or even thought of. Don't you worry."

What had all happened before she was born? Lottie thought frustratedly. Sometimes Uncle Jack seemed to think she was about five. She was not to worry? As if that was going to happen.

Sofie stretched and yawned and stepped delicately off her cushion. "I feel *much* better," she announced. "Did I miss anything? Are these mice exciting? Striped, perhaps?" She gave a dismissive sniff.

Giles bowed to her. "I am afraid I am not a mouse." He peered down at his stomach admiringly. "You could get about three mice out of me, I should think. Were you expecting mice? Am I in the wrong place?" He brushed his whiskers worriedly with one paw and looked apologetically at Uncle Jack.

"Well, possibly. . . My order was actually for some rather interesting Russian blue mice, but you are really most welcome to stay. We specialize in mice, but I would be delighted to make the proper acquaintance of a hamster." Uncle Jack and Giles bowed to each other gravely again and Lottie began to think that the manners of everyone in the shop were about to undergo a serious improvement in order to live up to Giles's standards.

She left Uncle Jack and Giles exchanging polite small talk and beckoned to Sofie to follow her upstairs. Sofie had lived with Uncle Jack for a while – he had bought her several years before as a present for his wife. Lottie thought Sofie had been rather lonely since her aunt had died, which was why she'd been ready to be Lottie's familiar. Perhaps Sofie knew what Uncle Jack wasn't telling her.

"What is the matter?" Sofie asked as soon as they were curled up on Lottie's bed. Then she sniffed hopefully. "Wait a minute, have you got any chocolate left? I can smell violet creams." She peered meaningfully at Lottie's bedside table.

Lottie fetched out the box and waited until Sofie was blissfully licking her lips in case she'd missed any. There was no point in talking to her while she was in the middle of a chocolate.

"Mmm. French chocolate. So obviously superior." Sofie opened her eyes at last and looked enquiringly at Lottie. "So. What is it, dear Lottie?"

"A horrible person's being horrible to her!" Fred popped his pink nose out of Lottie's school cardigan, making her jump. She'd forgotten he was there. "Have you got chocolate for me too?" he asked hopefully.

Lottie sighed and handed over another violet cream, plus another one for Sofie because she looked so mournful. It was probably a good thing that the animals ate so many – her mother tended to send her lots of chocolates and presents from Paris, because she felt guilty about being away. If Lottie had eaten them all she'd be the size of a house.

"What sort of horrible person?" Sofie asked at last.

"An enchantreth," Fred mumbled, his mouth smeared with chocolate. The violet cream was about the size of his head and he was making it last.

"I beg your pardon?" Sofie demanded frostily. She liked to make her position as Lottie's familiar and confidante clear by

32

bossing the mice around as much as possible.

"An enchantreth! Enchantreth! Bad witf! Oh, askth Lottie!" Fred took another nibble of chocolate.

"It was an enchantress," Lottie told her quietly.

Sofie blinked. "That one who came before?" she asked sharply and Lottie nodded.

"Giles, that new hamster, met her while she was buying two dogs, salukis I think he said. Have you heard of those?" Lottie had no idea what salukis were like.

Sofie sat up very straight, almost as though she were trying to make herself look taller.

"Nasty, rude, foreign dogs," she hissed.

Fred looked up. "*You're* foreign!" he pointed out.

"*I* am French," Sofie replied coldly. She clearly thought this made sense.

"Well, I thought they must be," Lottie agreed. "I've never heard of them though. Where do they come from?"

33

"Egypt," Sofie muttered huffily. "Oldest dogs in the world, supposedly. Royal dogs of the pharaohs. *Nonsense*. Mad as ferrets and too thin! Skinny!"

"Ohhhh." Lottie looked at Sofie, whose whiskers were positively vibrating with irritation. "Are they possibly quite . . . tall?"

"Maybe," Sofie spat. "Perhaps a little taller than me. But not much!" she added fiercely, glaring at Lottie.

"No, of course not," Lottie agreed. Sofie was so cross that she wasn't controlling her thoughts and a picture of a saluki was shimmering on Lottie's bedroom wall. It was a beautiful dog, a light creamy golden colour, with long feathery fur and a pointed nose. It looked like a very aristocratic greyhound. It also looked completely mad, but Lottie was pretty sure that was only because it was Sofie's imagination that was in control. She could see why the saluki upset Sofie. It did have *very* long legs.

The saluki raced off into the distance, past Lottie's pink spotty curtains, and Sofie huffed crossly. "So, she has got herself two mad dogs. Huh."

Lottie looked at her thoughtfully. "Sofie, do you know anything about that enchantress that you haven't told me? Had you met her before? Uncle Jack knows her but he won't tell me why."

Sofie glanced up in surprise, the salukis forgotten at last. "No! He has not said. . . I had not seen her before she came to the shop that day – all I know is that she was evil. You could tell. She made the air taste bad." Sofie shivered.

"He said it was all to do with before I was born." Lottie stared round her bedroom, the pretty curtains, the spotted bedcover, the pink fairy mirror. She wished she could remember more about her life at the shop when she was tiny. She had lived here with her parents when her dad and Uncle Jack ran the shop together.

But after her dad had died, her mum had left, too sad to stay and be reminded of him every day. She had never understood the magic of the shop and she knew nothing about Lottie's powers. Lottie wasn't sure she would ever be able to tell her – she just wasn't the kind of person who believed in magic.

Lottie sighed. She wished she knew more about her father too. He was a strange shadowy figure in her life, only a memory from photographs. Lottie was never sure whether she really remembered those times, or whether she'd simply imagined them from the few flat, bright pictures she had. Uncle Jack had given her a photo album with loads more pictures in it. Her and Danny playing in a paddling pool while he and her father watched them, laughing. They looked so alike. Lottie tried so hard to remember but she'd only been tiny then. She'd tried to ask Danny if he remembered but he denied it in disgust. He also said that if she ever let anyone see that photo he would pour treacle in her hair.

She couldn't help feeling closer to her father here, where he'd lived too. A place he'd loved. And Uncle Jack was his image, just a little greyer, as it was eight years since those photos had been taken. She just wanted to know so much more about him. Uncle Jack didn't seem to want to tell her much. He'd happily look at the photos with her and tell her what a sweet little girl she'd been, but if she started to ask about her father's magic or where he'd gone on that last journey, Uncle Jack would change the subject and then suddenly remember an urgent delivery he had to make. Lottie tried to remember that it had to be hard for Uncle Jack too – her dad was his brother, after all. But why did he have to be so secretive about him?

When her mother had last come to visit, Lottie had forced her to tell more than she ever had before about her father. Lottie still felt the tiniest bit guilty because it had upset her mum to remember. But not that guilty. Her mum had refused to talk about her father for so long, Lottie reckoned she had a right to know.

Her mum was still angry. She hadn't wanted Lottie's dad to go on the trip to the rainforests, and leave her and Lottie, and she'd thought he was mad when he suggested they came too. Lottie found it hard to understand how they'd ever fallen in love and got married. They were so different! Mum was so sensible and cautious and desperate to look after Lottie by making sure she worked hard and earned enough. From everything everyone said, Lottie's dad wouldn't have cared where they lived and what they had to eat, as long as they were happy. And that wasn't even mentioning the fact that he had magic! How could Mum never have known? Lottie still found it impossible to believe. But then, Mum always had a sensible explanation for anything odd that happened. She was just like all the non-magical people who came into the shop – their eyes just seemed to slide over anything odd.

"I am sorry, Lottie," Sofie said gently, nosing at her arm. "I know you hate all this secrecy about your father. I promise you, I do not know what your uncle is hiding."

Lottie stroked her smooth head gently. "It's all right, I know." She closed her eyes for a moment and let Sofie's comforting furry thoughts fill her head. They were almost equally split between love of chocolate and love of Lottie.

"Shall we go downstairs?" Sofie suggested. "I would like to meet this hamster properly." Sofie felt it was her duty to interview any new arrivals at the shop. Lottie wondered if she and Giles would get on. They both seemed equally strong-minded and she could imagine them not being able to stand one another.

The stairs led straight into the shop and Lottie heard a familiar voice as they came down. Mr Fieldfare was back, talking earnestly to Uncle Jack, while his friend Mr Bucklebank wandered around the cages chirruping to the mice.

"It's most peculiar," Mr Fieldfare was saying worriedly. "Oh, hello, Leah."

Uncle Jack raised his eyebrows but Lottie made a "doesn't matter" face.

"Many of the artefacts she has in her windows are absolutely packed full of power. What if the wrong person bought them? It looks like one of those silly shops full of candles and crystals and getting your astrological chart drawn, whatever that is. But this stuff is far more dangerous. I just don't know what the owner can be thinking."

"It's definitely someone who knows what they've got?" Uncle Jack asked thoughtfully. "Not just a mistake? Someone who happened to collect all these things by chance."

Mr Fieldfare shook his head grimly. "No. It's a woman and she knows exactly what she's doing. Those windows are arranged to ensnare passers-by. She wants control, Jack – I don't know why. For its own sake, maybe. This is a busy town. Hundreds of people pass by those windows every day. Even if only one stops – imagine the harm she could do them!"

Uncle Jack anxiously shook his head.

Mr Bucklebank saw Lottie watching and smiled. "Someone has opened a magic shop," he told her in his low, musical voice. Lottie could imagine him bespelling people with a word – his voice thrummed with power. "Louis is most upset. He thinks it will upset the balance of everything in your pretty little town." He stroked a mouse's head gently with one finger and the mouse closed its eyes blissfully. "I'm not so sure."

"You think everything will be all right?" Lottie asked anxiously.

Mr Bucklebank gazed down at her. He really was extremely tall. "No. Not necessarily. But sometimes the balance ought to be upset, don't you think? Life would be rather boring otherwise." He tickled the mouse under the chin and it fell over backwards with its paws in the air, then struggled up, giggling. Sofie snorted with disgust. Mr Bucklebank chuckled. "Balance, Lottie," he pointed out. "Sometimes it's quite fun to fall over."

Lottie looked at him doubtfully, but he was tickling the mouse again and he seemed to think their conversation was over. Lottie wasn't so sure about being unbalanced. As someone who would have laughed herself silly only a few months ago if anyone had told her she was going to live in a magic pet shop, she couldn't imagine what would happen if the whole town suddenly found out that magic was real. The only person she had told was Ruby and that had been frightening enough. She *trusted* Ruby. How would Zara and her gang react to the news?

"Lottie, don't panic." Uncle Jack was staring at her, looking concerned.

"But what if everyone gets really angry?" Lottie whispered. She'd learned about witch burning in school – she knew it had all happened a long time ago but she could just imagine Zara tying her to a stake.

"Do you remember what I said to you when you wanted to tell Ruby about the shop?" Uncle Jack asked her gently.

Lottie tried to think back, but eventually she shook her head apologetically.

"People have an amazing ability not to see things," Uncle Jack explained. "Like your mother."

"Oh, yes." Lottie remembered now. "Only the right people would understand. But you said that Ruby might not want to be friends with me any more," she added slowly.

"Exactly. She would always have felt that there was something strange about you, even if she couldn't quite put her finger on it. She wouldn't have trusted you." Uncle Jack sighed. "That's what Louis and I are worried about.

Not mobs descending on us with flaming torches — no, I'm not reading your mind, Lottie, it's just obvious what you're thinking." He smiled sadly at her. "No, I've lived here so long. We belong here, our family. If people are suddenly suspicious about us, even if they don't know why, all that will be spoilt. This is my home. I don't want to leave."

"I don't want to either!" Lottie gasped out. And it was true. Netherbridge felt more like home than the flat where she'd lived with her mother. Sofie nudged her leg lovingly with a damp nose. Lottie had promised her that she would never go back there and leave her behind, but Sofie still couldn't help worrying about it. How could Lottie choose between Sofie and her own mother?

"If this new shop starts letting out all our secrets, life is going to be very difficult," Louis Fieldfare said grimly.

"Can't you stop it?" Lottie asked, looking back and forth between them anxiously.

Uncle Jack held out his hands in a despairing gesture. "How? We can't force this woman to close down. We've no power." He sighed. "Perhaps people just won't want to buy these things," he muttered.

Mr Fieldfare gave a bitter laugh. "It may be dangerous magic but it's disguised as love charms and fortune telling. She'll be run off her feet." He sank glumly on to a stool by the counter.

"Cheer up, Louis." Mr Bucklebank came in from the back room where he'd been admiring Uncle Jack's lizards. One of them was perched on his hat. "Tell Jack about your discovery."

Mr Fieldfare smiled and shook his head. "Jacob thinks I'm imagining things but I know I saw it. We went for a walk – the scenery here is so pretty, you know, and Jacob had never been to Netherbridge. And you'll never guess what we saw! A unicorn! Up on Netherbridge Hill of all places."

Uncle Jack went pale. It was quite shocking to watch — all the colour simply drained out of his face, leaving it dead white beneath his grizzled black hair.

"Oh! Oh, Jack, I'm sorry. I had forgotten." Mr Fieldfare reached out and put a hand on his arm.

"Not in front of. . ." Uncle Jack waved a hand at Lottie who was staring at them in amazement.

"No, no of course not. No, indeed." Mr Fieldfare worriedly stared at her.

"What is it?" Lottie begged, but Uncle Jack shook his head.

"Nothing. Nothing at all. An old memory, Lottie." He rubbed a hand over his face wearily. "Lottie, I need some fresh air. A quick walk. You and Sofie could mind the shop for me for half an hour, couldn't you? Danny should be home soon anyway."

Lottie nodded unwillingly. She knew he wouldn't tell her any more. Her uncle had an amazing ability to slide out from under questions. Danny had inherited it. Conversations with both of them could be like walking on shifting sand.

She watched as the three men hurried out of the shop. She was pretty certain where they were going.

Straight up to Netherbridge Hill.

Lottie got out her homework and sat at the counter staring at it, with Sofie on her lap. Giles the hamster was having a restorative nap in his new cage and had resolutely refused to wake up and be examined, even when Sofie gave him one of her best stares. This was impressive as Sofie's stares could probably wake the dead. Sofie was most irritated and was taking it out on Lottie's homework by being very rude about her mock newspaper article.

The door clanged loudly and Lottie sat up with her best helpful smile. She hoped whoever it was didn't actually want to buy anything as she hated using the cash register – it always bit her.

Sofie growled. A long, low whisper of a growl that woke every animal in the shop and put them on their guard immediately. It was a growl that meant *enemy*.

The mice buried themselves in their bedding with panicked squeaks, and even Selina and Sarafan watched nervously from their pen, tails twitching.

Lottie looked at the door hopefully. Surely Uncle Jack would be back soon? Wasn't it almost half an hour? And where on earth was Danny when she needed him?

But there was no one there to help her. The white-haired enchantress in the red dress, the one who had some strange history with Lottie that she didn't understand, the one that Giles had heard making odd threats, was now standing in front of the counter. Smiling.

"Lottie! How charming!" Her voice was like a peal of silvery bells, clear, sweet, insistent.

Irresistible.

Lottie gulped and closed her eyes for a second, slamming shut all the doors in her mind.

The enchantress's smile showed more teeth. "That isn't very friendly, Lottie," she cooed. "Can't we talk, at least? You owe me that, don't you, after you shut me out of your mind so harshly when I was here last. That was rather rude, Lottie dear. Not many people are rude to me. I can't quite decide what to do about you. Really, of course, I should just crush every thought you own so that you can never think again." Her voice was light and almost laughing, but it wasn't a joke.

She came closer and leaned against the counter, idly drawing circles on its dusty surface with a perfect fingernail. "But then, that might be a little short-sighted. There's something so interesting about a powerful new mind." She looked at Lottie for a moment, her head on one side, as though she was trying to decide on something terribly important, like which cake to have for tea. Lottie had the awful feeling that the enchantress was mad enough to think destroying her would be the same kind of decision.

Then she smiled suddenly, her eyes glinting. She seemed to be running down a different track now. "I'm your new neighbour, Lottie, did you know?" she asked. "I've bought a little shop, just down the road. A little gift shop. I shall be keeping it much the same, with just the tiniest alterations in the stock here and there. Slightly *different* presents. I'm sure they'll have a most interesting effect. I should think that lots of your friends from school would enjoy a visit. Perhaps you could tell them about me?"

Lottie could feel the fear radiating from every animal in the shop. Sofie was snuggled in to her as close as she could go, her nose pressed into the crook of Lottie's elbow, trembling.

What is it about her that's so scary? Lottie wondered. *Why are we all so frightened?* Having the terrified thoughts of hundreds of tiny creatures in her head was making her feel worse than ever. She couldn't stop watching the enchantress's fingers, drawing those patterns on the dusty counter. Such a silly thing to do. Irritating, really. Lottie wished she'd stop. For some strange reason, the patterns were starting to make her feel dizzy.

"Hem–hem!"

Lottie blinked and shook the fuzzy feeling out of her head.

Giles the hamster marched smartly across the counter (Lottie could almost hear the brass band thumping away inside her head, definitely a military tune) and took up a defensive position in front of her. He plumped his rather large bottom down and glared at the enchantress.

She laughed. "This little mouse is protecting you, Lottie dear! How perfectly sweet."

"I am not a mouse, madam," Giles replied icily. "I am a hamster. There are significant differences. Note the lack of a tail."

The enchantress raised her eyebrows slightly and stared at him. She clearly expected him to collapse into a quivering heap, but Giles just stared back. He was like a slightly grumpy little old man, Lottie thought, glaring at a group of bratty children. He seemed completely unafraid of the enchantress's magic.

She frowned and Lottie noticed how much less beautiful it made her. Her face was so perfect, until it was spoiled by frown lines and a pouting underlip. She no longer looked as though she were made of some precious stone – she was human and irritated. Suddenly she was much less frightening.

The enchantress raised a hand, as though to point a spell at Giles. Lottie wasn't sure whether she would actually dare to do it. Last time she had been to the shop she'd clearly had a healthy respect for Uncle Jack, so killing one of his creatures might not be a wise move. But Lottie wasn't taking any chances. She snatched Giles up and held him close against her. Sofie growled a warning and all three of them stared at the enchantress.

"For future reference, Lottie dear, mind the fur," Giles muttered.

"Sorry. . ." Lottie could feel some of his unshakeable confidence seeping into her fingers. She felt much better already.

The enchantress looked down at her fingers, almost worriedly, as though she thought something might be wrong with them. Lottie could almost hear her thinking, *Why can't I just squash them? A little girl and a fussy little dog and a hamster?*

We don't believe in her any more, Lottie realized, as she saw the mice creeping towards the bars of their cages curiously. *We don't believe she'll do all these awful things.* Then a sudden thought hit her and she gave a tiny gasp. *And that makes her all the more dangerous,*

*now she's got something to prove. She'll want to
have us back the way we were before. She's going to
squish my mind!*

At that moment, the door clanged again and
Uncle Jack walked in, looking considerably
better than he had half an hour ago.

"You!" he snapped, his dark eyes flashing.

The enchantress wheeled round and backed
against the counter, looking almost hunted.

"Get out of my shop, Pandora. Leave my
niece alone."

"Your . . . niece. . ." The enchantress
blinked at him, clearly thinking fast.

"Yes. She's not mine. Is that what you
thought? No. This is Tom's girl." Uncle Jack
folded his arms, looking down at her almost
triumphantly.

She bit her lip, staring at Lottie, her small
white teeth actually cutting into the skin
leaving a tiny bead of blood. Then she plunged
out of the shop, the door swinging to behind
her with a sigh.

Lottie slumped against the counter and Giles stepped out of her hands and strolled over towards Uncle Jack.

"More sunflower seeds, do you think, old chap?"

Chapter 3

Lottie stood up, her legs shaking slightly. She was still hugging Sofie tight, grateful for the feel of soft fur under her fingers. She waited until Uncle Jack had finished pouring out a generous bowl of sunflower seeds for Giles, then she caught his eye as he looked up. He looked at her, apologetic and rather embarrassed.

"I'm not going to get away with it this time, am I, Lottie?"

"Who *is* she?" Lottie demanded. "You know it's her who's bought the shop down the road, the one that Mr Fieldfare was so upset about?"

"I did wonder," Uncle Jack admitted. "She's not going to be easy to get rid of." He sighed. "Her name is Pandora Gold. She's a witch. Just like Ariadne."

Lottie snorted. "No, she isn't. Ariadne said that before, that *she* could have been just like that, and it all depended on what you did. She was trying to warn me about not doing the wrong things with my magic. There's no way Ariadne could be like that. That woman's evil!"

Uncle Jack nodded. "Absolutely. But she's made herself evil, Lottie. You don't get born a bad witch. You're made. Mostly by yourself." He paused. "Pandora turned . . . a few years ago. She was always a little too interested in controlling other people's minds, but she would at least convince herself that she had good reasons for it. She went away after that – she used to live in Netherbridge, you see – and I don't know what she's been doing the last few years. Stuff I'd rather not think about."

Lottie waited for him to say more, but he was watching Giles stuff his cheek pouches and carefully not looking at her. "Uncle Jack! What about the rest?"

Uncle Jack glanced up at her, blinked and tried to look innocent. He only managed shifty. He looked very like Danny. "The rest?"

"Why is she interested in me? She said it was because she couldn't get in my mind, but there's something else, isn't there? When you told her I wasn't your daughter, she looked like she'd swallowed a hedgehog. What is it? Tell me!"

Uncle Jack's eyes were full of hurt as he stared back at her. "I can't, Lottie. I promised. It isn't my story to tell."

"So who *will* tell me?" Lottie wailed.

Uncle Jack wandered away into the storeroom. "Only Pandora could tell you the whole story," he whispered bitterly. "The only other person who knows is dead."

Lottie went to bed early that night. Danny had finally got home from school late after football practice, which he hadn't told anyone he had. At least it cheered Uncle Jack up – he'd been worrying about how much Danny hated school and knowing that Danny had joined a team made him feel much better. Septimus was less keen, or he pretended he was. If Danny could actually be bothered to do any magic, Septimus was his familiar and he adored Danny, even though he told him off constantly. He had to stay in the changing room during football, hiding in Danny's kitbag, and he complained about it bitterly. "The smell!" he moaned faintly to Sofie at the dinner table. "It's still on my fur. I may have to sleep on a lavender bag tonight."

Sofie edged to the other side of her chair and continued delicately sucking spaghetti.

"I'm watching the match tonight, OK?" Danny told Lottie. "You can watch too, if you like," he added graciously.

"I'd rather die," Lottie muttered. She was still edgy from her encounter that afternoon and she didn't want to spend the evening with Danny lecturing her on football. "I think I preferred you when you hated everything. All this football stuff is really boring."

"You should get more exercise, Lottie," Danny told her pityingly, waving his fork at her. "Then you wouldn't be so moody. It's all to do with low energy levels, you know."

"If you watch this football with him, I will never speak to you again," Sofie told Lottie with a string of spaghetti dangling from one side of her mouth. She slurped it up with a satisfying squelch and everyone shuddered. Considering she was a dog, Sofie normally ate very tidily, but spaghetti was not her strong point.

Lottie climbed the stairs to her room with Sofie after dinner. She was planning to listen to some music and maybe read a bit. She'd asked Giles if he wanted to come, but he'd gracefully declined, saying that the afternoon had worn him out. When she passed his cage after dinner he was invisible under a pile of hay bedding which was very gently rising and falling with his snores.

Lottie sympathized. She was exhausted too. She put her radio on and lay on her bed reading a magazine with Sofie beside her, but she kept blinking.

"If my boyfriend kept staring at other girls, I would bite him," Sofie suggested, reading the *Love Letters* page. She kept snorting disgustedly.

"Mmm. She should definitely dump him," Lottie yawned. "Oh, Sofie, I'm so sleepy. The enchantress – I know she's called Pandora but I can't think of her as anything except the enchantress still – she wore me out, I think. I felt like I was holding her out of my head the whole time she was here. She was like water trying to seep through the cracks."

"Me as well." Sofie nodded. "And the badness! She made me feel sick. She is a monster, that one."

Lottie didn't answer. She had been leaning on her arms, staring at the magazine, but now her head had slipped sideways. Sofie nudged her gently so that she wouldn't get a crick in her neck and tugged the magazine out from under Lottie's cheek with her teeth. Then she burrowed herself lovingly under Lottie's arm and went to sleep too. Lottie felt her closeness and sighed softly in her sleep, wriggling herself comfortable. They were warm and weary and safe.

Lottie stopped walking and looked back down over the little town. The path up Netherbridge Hill was steep and slippery, and it was nearly dark. The streetlights were just starting to come on below her and Netherbridge looked cosy and welcoming, surrounded by hills, with the river snaking through and reflecting the amber lights in its dark water.

Lottie sighed, wishing they could go back home and drink hot chocolate with marshmallows in the shop with Uncle Jack. She even took one or two steps back down the path, but she couldn't. They had to go on and find the unicorn. She knew it was important somehow, in that weird way one knows things in dreams—

"Lottie, is this a dream?" Sofie demanded curiously.

"Oh! Yes, it must be. . ." Lottie looked around her. Everything seemed very real. She had been up Netherbridge Hill once before, a few weeks ago, with Ruby. It had been a sunny weekend – they'd taken a picnic and lain about on the sweet-smelling grass, gossiping about school.

Now it was chilly and the hills seemed steeper and craggier. Lottie shivered. It was getting darker every moment and a gusty wind was blowing. If there was a unicorn up here, there might be other things too. . .

"Lottie, where are we going?" Sofie asked plaintively. "We have come a *very* long way."

Lottie gave her a surprised look. "The dream only started a minute ago. We've come about fifty metres, that's all!"

Sofie shook her head. "No, we've walked all the way up, I am sure." She wrinkled her nose. "Well, it feels as if we have."

Lottie scooped her up, glad of her warm weight anyway. The hill was very lonely and strangely quiet.

"Do you know where we are going?" Sofie asked again.

"Only that we're going to find a unicorn," Lottie told her, hoping she wouldn't start laughing.

"Oh! The one that Louis Fieldfare saw. He is a silly man, Lottie. He may have made it up. His unicorn might be no more than a rabbit with a white tummy."

"I know. But did you see the way Uncle Jack reacted when Mr Fieldfare told him about it? It was like he got ten years older all of a sudden. He knows something about unicorns, Sofie. And Mr Fieldfare knew about it too – he remembered when Uncle Jack looked so ill.

He was really sorry he'd said it. I was going to ask Uncle Jack about it, but then the enchantress came and she made me forget everything else."

"Mmm." Sofie looked thoughtful. "Dreams are good for remembering the important things. I do not know if unicorns are real, Lottie. I think they were once. But now – they may all be lost."

"Uncle Jack knew something about them. I'm positive he did." Lottie smiled excitedly. "After all, Sam and Joe – Ruby's lizards – say that they're dragons and that their cousins are much bigger. So if dragons are real, why not unicorns?"

Sofie nodded consideringly. "Perhaps." Then her ears pricked up slightly, a sharper look coming into her eyes. "Lottie, can you hear something?"

"No-ooo, I don't think so." Lottie looked around anxiously. "Only the wind. Why, what can you hear?"

"Footsteps." Sofie peered grimly down the path behind them. "*Paws*. Large ones. Someone's coming, and they're trying not to let us hear."

"This is still only a dream, isn't it?" Lottie asked nervously. Being chased in the dark by something large with paws was making her think that actually it was more of a nightmare.

Sofie glanced up at her quickly. "I do not know. Dreams can be real too."

Lottie gulped. "Can we wake ourselves up?"

Sofie blinked. Then she shook her head. "No. Or at least, I cannot. Can you?"

Lottie shrugged helplessly. "No. Most of me thinks I already am awake. I don't know how." She shuddered. "Oh, Sofie, it's her isn't it? Pandora?"

"Yes. . . And I think she has with her those dogs, the ones Giles told you about. They run very fast, Lottie. They do not ever stop until they have brought down their prey." Sofie was tense in Lottie's arms. "It would be better not to run," she admitted reluctantly.

"You mean we just have to stand here and wait for them to catch us?" Lottie gasped.

Sofie looked at her unhappily. "We cannot escape. And it is, perhaps, only a dream after all."

"It isn't," Lottie said grimly. "I can tell. She's down there, real as anything. What does she *want*? Oh, I wish Uncle Jack wasn't so cagey, then at least we'd know what we were dealing with."

"Has Ariadne taught you anything that might help?" Sofie asked hopefully.

Lottie thought frantically. "Only those same closed-mind spells I used against Pandora before. I've done those really carefully. But mostly we've been working on finding my magic and keeping it under control. It's since you and I accidentally went into a trance and chased Zara's mind, that night after we first found our magic, when Fred and Peach had to bite me. Ariadne wanted me to know how to control the power and channel it, so we didn't get carried away."

"I think right now we should get carried away as much as possible," Sofie said grimly.

Lottie could hear them now. Scufflings and panting breaths, and an excited voice urging the dogs on in an angry whisper.

"Back up against the rock, Lottie," Sofie whispered. "We do not want those dogs behind us."

They flattened themselves against the rock wall that lined one side of the path. Lottie tried hard not to look scared. A lot of Pandora's magic was all show, she was sure. It was about telling people they were frightened so that they would be.

Pandora seemed to shine as she glided up the path. A soft yellow glow outlined her and she looked angelic.

"Tacky," Sofie muttered.

Lottie smiled. Thank goodness for Sofie. *She* had been thinking it was rather impressive and wondering how she could do anything against such strong magic. Tacky was a much more useful way to look at it.

Pacing on either side of the enchantress were two enormous dogs. They were very beautiful, one a golden brown colour, and one black. Their feathery fur shone in their mistress's magical light and they ran so gracefully that they seemed to float along beside her.

Sofie hissed angrily to herself and Lottie held her tightly. She could tell that Sofie was scared – she could feel Sofie's velvety-black fear pulsing in her own head. But Sofie was so proud that she might try to show that she wasn't frightened by leaping at one of the salukis. They might be beautiful, but their jaws looked fierce, and the two of them could probably have little Sofie for a light snack. Not that she would ever admit it.

The enchantress stopped an arm's length from Lottie and smiled kindly at her. It made

Lottie's skin crawl. She stared back, forcing herself not to lower her eyes.

"Dearest Lottie," Pandora purred. "How lovely to meet you here. Such a happy coincidence. It's the most charming walk, isn't it? My favourite walk round here. I lived in Netherbridge before, you know, some years ago. I expect your uncle told you? About our . . . history?"

Lottie shook her head and Sofie whispered, "Coincidence!" in a disbelieving voice.

Pandora moved a step closer. "And even before I knew who you were, Lottie, I couldn't let a mind like yours get away. So rude, you know, to block someone out of your mind like that, the way you did when I first met you." She frowned for a moment. "But such power, Lottie. Such potential. A real waste that Ariadne is teaching you. I could do far more with a mind like yours than that feeble herb-gatherer. Do think about it. While you can." She smiled seductively, but her eyes were watchful. "No? Well, anyway, now that I am back amongst my old haunts, I love to exercise my dogs here. Prosper, Fatima, this is Lottie, with her own dear little dog. Lottie is a friend so you are not to chase the poor little thing."

Lottie clutched Sofie in a death grip, knowing that she was desperate to leap for the enchantress's throat. Why was she being so horribly friendly now? Did she really want Lottie for an apprentice? Lottie felt like screaming, *I'm not your friend! I never want to learn anything from you!*

The salukis eyed Sofie watchfully. They looked hungry and twitchy, as though they would be delighted to chase down anyone who put so much as a foot out of place.

If we could wake up, now would be a very good time. . . Sofie said in her head.

I'm trying! Lottie promised her, but Pandora's cooing voice was wrapping round her, coating her mind in syrup. Uncle Jack loved to put golden syrup on pancakes, Lottie thought, smiling to herself. He would let Lottie mess around with the sweet-smelling tin, trickling the syrup off a fork and letting it smooth itself out into a golden lake. . .

Syrup? Why on earth was she thinking about syrup? Her mind back under control, Lottie jumped, and screamed out loud. Pandora was right next to her, one hand on the rocky wall, the other reaching for Lottie's throat, and her face was like stone.

"This is a dream!" Lottie yelled and smacked Pandora in the face as hard as she could.

The enchantress gasped, stepping back and putting a hand to her cheek in shock. But her shock didn't last long. The full force of Pandora's mind hit Lottie in seconds and it felt as if the rock wall had collapsed on her head.

Lottie whimpered, and worst of all, she could hear Sofie whimpering in the darkness too. She tried desperately to fight back, but Pandora was hammering at her thoughts and Lottie could feel that syrup seeping into the corners of her mind. Pandora was filling her head, forcing Lottie out.

Help me! she wailed, not sure who she was crying to. She was watching the horrible, triumphant smile on the enchantress's face, miserably waiting for her to do whatever it was she was planning when she won. Was she going to steal Lottie's mind somehow? Enslave her? She said apprentice, but Lottie was sure she meant slave. . .

Suddenly the smile faltered. Lottie blinked. What was happening?

What is that noise? Sofie hissed silently.

You're there! Lottie hugged her even tighter. She hadn't been able to feel Sofie since the enchantress had attacked.

Of course I am! Do not squeeze me like that. Something else is coming. And she is afraid of it. Look at her.

Lottie looked up at Pandora. She was gazing out at the hillside behind Lottie with an angry, frightened expression. The dogs were weaving around her nervously and she snapped at them.

At last Lottie heard it, what Sofie's sensitive ears had caught ages before. The thudding of hooves on the hard ground.

Lottie gasped. The unicorn! It had to be. She was so excited that she swung round to see, ignoring the enchantress entirely.

Galloping towards them was an enormous silver-white creature, his coat gleaming in the moonlight. He raced across the ground, making for the rocky wall behind Lottie and Sofie, and swung himself to a skidding stop on top of the crag, his hooves striking sparks from the stone. Then he put his head down, swinging his enormous horn in between Lottie and Pandora, and growled, "Leave her."

"I shan't – you can't—" Pandora started to protest, but the unicorn's swiftly indrawn breath sent her stumbling backwards.

"You will. . . *Or else*," said the deep snarling voice. It was frightening, that voice, but strangely familiar. It made Lottie feel safe. She couldn't help feeling that she must have met this unicorn before. But she couldn't have.

Pandora staggered away, her dogs glancing back fearfully, their tails hanging low as the unicorn watched them go.

Then he leaped gracefully down on to the narrow path, landing perfectly beside Lottie.

"Show-off," Sofie muttered. She wasn't grateful to be rescued.

The unicorn snorted with amusement and nudged her affectionately with his nose. "Take good care of her, little one," he whispered, then he turned and galloped away up the path, a flash of white disappearing in the darkness.

Then Lottie woke up.

Lottie shivered, for the room was cold and dark now. She supposed Uncle Jack must have come to check on her and turned off her light. She sat up and Sofie wriggled into her arms. She was trembling too.

"Sofie, was — was that a dream? Or did it really happen? It seemed so real!" Lottie whispered shakily.

"It happened," Sofie muttered. "I don't know how she got us there, but she must have done. She wanted to bind our minds, Lottie, to tie us to her. Make us hers. All that sweetness, that syrupiness — she was seeping in. And as soon as she had made it she would have done something awful. Though I am not entirely sure what."

Lottie shuddered. "She asked if I wanted to be her apprentice. I think she was trying to make us hers somehow — whether we wanted it or not. I can't imagine anything worse. I'd rather she killed us, Sofie. I know that's mad. But just think what she might make us do."

"I do not want to think about it." Sofie shook her ears briskly.

"Where did that unicorn come from?" Lottie wondered. "He turned up just in time — I called out for someone to help, but I

76

was hoping Uncle Jack or Ariadne or Danny would hear me somehow. I didn't expect a unicorn."

Sofie looked thoughtful. "It was not a unicorn."

"Sofie, it was! What else could it have been? It looked just like one! And it talked!" Lottie gazed at her feeling almost hurt. Sofie had been there. How could she deny it now?

"It looked like a unicorn. But it was a dream creature, I am sure. Someone who loves you sent it to save you."

Lottie sat up. "Uncle Jack! It has to be. Like I said when we were in the dream, he looked awful when Mr Fieldfare mentioned unicorns. He must know something about them. I bet it was him." She got up, feeling her way carefully to the door. "There's still a light on downstairs, I can see it under the door. Let's go and find him."

They crept down the stairs to find Uncle Jack sitting at the counter, sucking his pencil and trying to work out the shop accounts.

"Lottie! Are you all right? Did you just wake up? I wasn't sure if I should wake you, but you looked so tired." Uncle Jack peered closer at her. "What's the matter? You look dreadful."

"Pandora chased us. She tried to bind us to her." Lottie slumped on to a stool next to him.

Uncle Jack put his pencil down and grabbed her arms. "What? I thought you were asleep upstairs!"

"We were. She was in my head. In my dream."

"Oh! You mean you had a nightmare. . ." Uncle Jack sounded relieved.

"No!" Sofie yapped sharply.

Lottie shrugged. "Well . . . yes. I guess so. But it was real too. So, it wasn't you then? I was sure it was," she muttered. "Especially after you got so upset about the unicorn before."

"What wasn't me? Lottie, you have to tell me what's going on!" Uncle Jack was looking really worried again.

"We were up on Netherbridge Hill, in the dream, looking for a unicorn. Then Pandora turned up and she nearly got in my head, Uncle Jack, she was so strong. But . . . a unicorn chased her away. . ." Lottie tailed off. It sounded so stupid.

"Like I said, Lottie, it was not a unicorn," Sofie said impatiently. "Somebody sent it to rescue us. It felt like you," she told Uncle Jack, in a considering tone.

"It wasn't," Uncle Jack said. "Listen, you two. There's something you need to know. Lottie, when your dad went off on that last trip, he wasn't just looking for exotic animals." Uncle Jack sighed. "He went to find unicorns, Lottie. He was obsessed with them and he'd heard rumours of unicorns off in the deep rainforests somewhere. That's why I was so upset. Unicorns make me think of how much I miss Tom – and how much you've missed by not having him around."

"Oh," Lottie said quietly. She wasn't sure what to think. It was nice to know something more about her father, but at the same time, he'd abandoned her and her mum to go off chasing unicorns in a rainforest. Even though Lottie had seen one – or at least a dream one – unicorns still felt like a fairy story. Something that a grown-up ought not to bother about. "I suppose we should go back to bed," she said wearily.

"Lottie!" Giles was looking down at her from the open door of his cage.

"Hi Giles. Is your cage nice?" Lottie asked him, managing a small smile.

"Lottie, you can't go back to sleep," Giles told her urgently.

Lottie stared at him, then realized he was right, of course. "What if she comes back! What are we going to do?" Suddenly she was desperate to sleep, this minute.

"Ariadne will have to teach you a way to guard your mind while you're sleeping," Uncle

Jack agreed. "But until then. . ."

"Until then, Lottie will have my cage in her room," Giles said calmly. "Hamsters are nocturnal. I shall be able to put in a spot of wheel running, keep myself trim. Any sign of a dream, enchantress or not, I shall jump on Lottie to wake her up." He smiled around at them modestly. "Do bear in mind that I am a trained battle hamster."

Chapter 4

"I was so sure it was Uncle Jack," Lottie muttered sleepily.

"Does it matter who it was, Lottie?" Giles asked her kindly. His cage was perched on her bedside table and he was already working out on his wheel. "Someone cares enough to send a dream creature to rescue you. That's a good thing."

Lottie nodded. "Yes, but I still want to know who it was!" She thought for a moment. "Oh, of course! Sofie, we're being stupid – it must have been Ariadne. I'm just too tired to think. I'll ask her about it tomorrow. We can go after school."

Sofie curled up under Lottie's chin. "I would have thought that Ariadne would send a cat. Shadow or Tabitha. Not a unicorn."

"Maybe Shadow and Tabitha weren't big enough. . ." Lottie yawned. "Go to sleep, Sofie. Goodnight, Giles."

Giles didn't bother to answer as Lottie was asleep already. He scurried round and round on his wheel, guarding them as they slept.

Ariadne's shiny, polished kitchen, with all its modern gadgets, seemed the last place to be talking about unicorns, but she was fascinated.

"You really saw one? There have been rumours of a unicorn up there for a while." She sighed. "I know it was an awful experience, Lottie, but you *are* lucky. There are people who'd give all of their teeth to have been there with you."

"And their mother's," Tabitha put in, smirking.

Sofie yapped with frustration. "I keep saying this! It was not a unicorn! It was a dream creature!"

Shadow, who had been curled on Ariadne's

lap, uncoiled himself and hissed, his near-blind eyes fixed on Sofie.

"Oh, do not be so bad-tempered," Sofie snapped. "Is no one allowed to disagree with your mistress? Pah."

"She knows a great more than you, little dog, about everything." Shadow's voice seemed to grow fainter every day, Lottie thought sadly.

"She does not because she was not there," Sofie retorted. "It was not a unicorn, it was a message that just looked like a unicorn."

"And if you didn't send it either, who was it?" Lottie demanded.

"It may not have been a flesh and blood unicorn," Ariadne told Sofie, "but it must have come from someone who had met one. You can't send that sort of magical image without knowing what you're doing. Think about that thought image you made of Zara. You couldn't have done it if you didn't know her, could you? In fact, Lottie, you probably couldn't have done it without her sitting there just because you haven't had that much practice at this sort of thing."

Lottie nodded. Ariadne was right.

"I wonder if the person who sent the unicorn to you has done it before – perhaps sent out the dream image to see Netherbridge while they're somewhere else? That would explain the other sightings," Ariadne mused.

"Like *spying*?" Lottie asked in surprise.

Ariadne looked up. "Well . . . I suppose so. I hadn't thought of it like that."

"It could be very useful," Sofie added thoughtfully.

"Right now we need to concentrate on spells to close your mind while you're sleeping," Ariadne reminded them. "Close your eyes, Lottie. . ."

The spells seemed to work – at least Lottie had no more strange dreams. But she couldn't help thinking that Pandora would not give up. She had been furious that Lottie had beaten her before, and knowing now that Lottie wasn't Uncle Jack's daughter apparently made it worse. Oh, if only Uncle Jack would tell her what was really going on!

Lottie had to walk past Pandora's shop every morning – she could have gone the other way up the street and along a bit, but that was stupid, and she wouldn't let anyone see that she was scared. It was horrible. Even Lottie, who knew hardly anything about magical artefacts, could see that this stuff was dangerous. In between the pretty china figures and the bead jewellery were *odd* things. Not obviously bad, just strange. But Lottie could see the deceptive magic tied to them. That funny little toy velvet cat, for example. Its bead eyes were definitely following her down the street every morning and she could hear its giggly purr in her head. *Buy me! Buy me! We'll have so much fun!* She hated to think what Pandora might have enchanted it to do.

She sped past this morning, trying not to look in the window. But a sudden movement behind the glass caught her eye and she glanced up without meaning to. Inside the shop, Pandora waggled her fingers in a teasing little wave. Lottie flushed scarlet. Pandora had been watching for her, had probably seen her before avoiding looking at the shop. She'd planned this and Lottie had done exactly what she wanted.

Made you look! The little velvet cat purred with delight and Lottie shuddered, racing off down the street.

Obviously Pandora hadn't given up. And Lottie was sure that she was planning something far, far worse than that. She had to be on her guard all the time. At least she was pretty sure that Pandora couldn't get at her at school. Not that she needed to. Zara Martin still did her best to make Lottie's life miserable the whole time she was there. She had discovered Pandora's shop already, which Lottie felt was just typical. She should have expected it, she supposed. Zara lived to shop and was always boasting about her shopping trips and the amount of money she'd made her mother spend. A couple of days ago she'd been flaunting a little china doll at school. It was beautiful, with china-fair skin, blue eyes, and dark hair – it looked exactly like Zara, spookily enough. The eyes moved, Lottie was prepared to swear to it. Zara was showing the doll off at lunch and, oddly, she'd shown it to Ruby. It had been almost as though she didn't want to. As though the doll had made her. There had been a puzzled expression in Zara's eyes as she muttered, "Ruby, have you seen this?" and her hands had moved jerkily as she held it out.

Ruby had reached over to stroke the doll's silken hair almost in a trance and Lottie had pulled her back, suddenly scared, but not fast enough to stop her touching it. It couldn't have hurt her, just a split-second's touch, could it?

Lottie was almost sure it couldn't, but it bothered her. She shuddered to think how many other people in Netherbridge had already bought things from Pandora's shop. And what the spells were making them do.

The woman in the sweet shop had been really off with her when she popped in to get some chocolate raisins for Giles and the pink mice yesterday. Usually she was friendly but she'd snapped at Lottie, telling her to stop hanging around the chocolate and that she needn't think she was getting away with nicking anything. She'd been twirling an odd glass necklace round and round her finger as she said it. Lottie couldn't blame everything that went wrong on Pandora (much as she'd like to) but the necklace looked awfully like one of the ones in Pandora's window.

Lottie dashed on to the bridge and looked around for Ruby. Oddly, she wasn't there. Ruby was almost always there waiting for her and Lottie wasn't particularly early today. She looked at her watch worriedly – in fact, she was almost late. Ruby had better hurry up – it was at least ten minutes' walk to school from here and that was all they had.

Five minutes later, Lottie gave up and started to run. Perhaps Ruby was ill? But surely she'd have called the shop and said? Ruby's mum knew they walked together – she'd have called, even if Ruby was too ill to do it. Feeling rather cross, Lottie dashed into school five minutes late and skidded into her seat just as Mrs Laurence started to take the register. Her teacher frowned disapprovingly and Lottie tried to look apologetic. She was having a hard time not looking furious as Ruby was in her usual place, right next to Lottie. From the look of her side of the table – pens neatly laid, a doodle already started in her homework diary – she'd been there a while.

"Where were you?" Lottie whispered crossly.

Ruby blinked and looked confused. "What

do you mean?"

"Why weren't you waiting for me at the bridge?" Lottie sounded hurt. How could Ruby have forgotten? But she was acting as though that was exactly what she'd done.

Ruby flushed pink, her freckles merging with the blush. "Oh, Lottie, I'm really sorry! I don't understand. . . That was so stupid. I just walked on my own like I used to. I'm sorry, did you wait for me?"

"Of course I did, and now Mrs Laurence's really cross!"

Luckily Mrs Laurence didn't stay cross with Lottie, but the morning was still miserable. Lottie felt really hurt that Ruby had forgotten her and Ruby was strange all day. Several times she seemed not to hear when Lottie said something and at lunch she started to walk to a table at the other end of the dining hall from where they usually sat.

"Ruby? Ruby! Where are you going?" Lottie tried to chase after her, nearly losing her plate of tomato pasta from her tray.

Ruby looked round vaguely, then her face cleared. "Oh, sorry Lottie, I wasn't thinking." And she headed back to their normal table.

By the end of the day, Lottie almost felt like she wasn't there. Ruby just seemed to keep forgetting about her. It was horrible. She didn't think Ruby was doing it on purpose – she seemed so surprised and apologetic every time she did it. But Lottie just couldn't believe the way she was behaving. She hadn't even had a chance to tell Ruby about Pandora in the shop this morning.

"So are you planning on walking back home with me today?" Lottie asked as they put their coats on. She felt a bit mean saying it, but she was cross. Maybe Ruby ought to see how upset she felt.

Ruby gave her a surprised look. "Oh, OK. Sure." And she walked out, swinging her bag over her shoulder.

Lottie stared after her, tears actually

stinging her eyes. Ruby hadn't meant to walk with her at all. She'd forgotten her again. This was awful. She followed a few steps behind Ruby, feeling embarrassed. She didn't want to be there if she wasn't wanted. She felt like she was getting on Ruby's nerves, being too friendly. Maybe Ruby just didn't like her any more. She was too nice to say it outright so she was just trying to back off from Lottie and make it obvious that way. Lottie hadn't felt this depressed since her mum had dumped her and swanned off to Paris – that was how it had felt at the time, anyway.

"Are you coming then?" Ruby called, turning round and walking backwards to look at Lottie. She didn't sound that bothered either way. Lottie half wanted to yell back that no, she wasn't, thanks very much, but she hated the thought of walking home on her own. She scurried after Ruby, desperately trying to think of something to say – to Ruby, her best friend, whom she could usually say whatever she liked to. They'd had a whole conversation last week when they just said the names of songs, and it was silly and mad and great. Now Ruby felt like a stranger.

Ruby sometimes popped into the pet shop on the way home from school with Lottie. It was out of her way but her mum didn't mind as long as she wasn't too late home. Lottie asked, trying to sound offhand about it, "You coming to the shop?"

"Mmmm." Ruby shrugged. And then they didn't say anything for ages.

They were just walking into Lottie's road when Ruby suddenly brightened up. "Oh, there's that new shop. I really want to get something for my mum for her birthday. They might have something a bit different. I'm just going to pop in there now."

"No!" Lottie gasped in horror. She really didn't want Pandora to meet Ruby. She had the most worrying feeling about it.

"Why not?" Ruby asked blankly, staring at

her. "Whatever's the matter with you, Lottie? You're being so weird today."

"Me. . .?" Lottie whispered, watching miserably as Ruby pushed open the shop door. The door bell rang with a sickeningly sweet chime. Lottie wanted desperately to run home but she couldn't leave Ruby there. She slunk after her, coughing a little as the door closed behind her – even the perfumed air of the shop seemed poisonous.

It was an eerie place. Lottie had got used to the way that when someone entered the pet shop, all the animals seemed to pause and hold their breath while they worked out whether they could keep talking or not. But she hadn't been expecting it to be the same here. A display of unpleasant-looking string puppets hanging on one wall had obviously stopped moving just as the bell rang. Lottie wondered if Ruby would notice that their arms and legs weren't floppy like they should be. Their painted eyes flicked from side to side as the girls moved into the shop and a nasty rustly whispering came from their scarlet-painted mouths.

That one. She knows. The other's an innocent. Don't move!

Was everything in the shop magical? She couldn't quite tell. Even the pretty china figurines that had belonged to the old lady who owned the shop before looked different now. Their sweet china faces seemed too pretty and the eyes were knowing.

There were some stranger things buried among the gifts. Odd musical instruments, carved wooden whistles and sets of pipes. Lottie wondered what they would call if she blew them, and shuddered.

Pandora was sitting behind the counter reading a little black-covered book. It looked unpleasant, as though it might be full of dark secrets.

"Lottie!" Pandora cooed. "And you've brought a friend. How lovely."

Ruby looked round in surprise. "You know

her?" she whispered.

Lottie opened her mouth but Pandora got in first. "You might say we're old family friends," she said smoothly.

Lottie stared at her with dislike but Pandora smiled back, seemingly amused.

"I'm looking for a birthday present for my mum," Ruby explained.

Pandora got up. "How nice. And did you have anything particular in mind?"

Ruby shook her head. "No, not really. She's quite hard to buy for. She likes unusual things. She's an artist."

"Oh, you've definitely come to the right place, Ruby." Pandora clapped her hands. "We have lots of unusual things."

Ruby blinked and stared at Pandora. "How did you know my name?"

"Well, you're a friend of Lottie's. I know an awful lot about Lottie, you see. And friends are so very, very important, wouldn't you agree?"

"I suppose. . ." Ruby faltered, but Pandora

97

wasn't looking at Ruby. She was staring at Lottie, her eyes like flint.

Lottie glared back. She was angry now. How dare the enchantress threaten her friends? Lottie looked over at Ruby, who was admiring some stone eggs in a bowl, and her heart jumped with fear. Not fear for herself but fear for Ruby. And guilt. Was she putting Ruby in danger by being friends with her? What if Pandora tried to do something to Ruby just to hurt Lottie? It seemed so unfair that Ruby should be dragged in when it wasn't even anything to do with her.

Then Lottie had a horrible thought. What if Pandora already had? She'd been thinking all day that Ruby had been acting weird and not like herself. They'd been best friends yesterday and today she was behaving like she hardly knew Lottie. Ruby wasn't the sort of person to bottle things up. If something Lottie had done had upset her, she'd say so. So why the sudden change?

It was as if someone had put a spell on her. . . The doll! Ruby had touched the doll! Could it really have enchanted her? Just that swift touch? It seemed unlikely but Lottie was sure the doll had something to do with this.

That's what Pandora's heavy hints were about. She'd bewitched Ruby and she wanted Lottie to know about it. Lottie looked up again and met Pandora's eyes, staring at her grimly. *I'll fight,* she whispered in her head, knowing that Pandora could hear. *You won't get her. I'll fight for her.*

Pandora smiled. *I know. . .*

Chapter 5

Lottie went back to the pet shop alone, feeling shaken. Ruby seemed to have forgotten she was supposed to be going to Lottie's – as they left Pandora's shop, she just turned the other way without even saying goodbye.

She hadn't bought anything for her mother – she said she needed to have a think and try sounding her mum out on what she wanted – but she'd bought a black felt cat for herself. As Ruby walked up the road, Lottie could see it sticking out of the pocket of her rucksack, grinning at her.

"What is wrong?" Sofie demanded as she walked in, trailing her schoolbag. "You look like you have seen a ghost. And there are no ghosts in this street, or I would have smelled them," she added matter-of-factly. "Not the unicorn again?"

Uncle Jack was selling sugar mice to Mrs Higgins for her two spoilt and bossy Siamese. He glanced worriedly over at Lottie and his customer smiled at her. "Bad day at school, Lottie?" she asked. "At least it's the weekend, dear. I'll bring you some of my special tea next time I'm in. That'll perk you right up."

Lottie managed to say something polite back and Mrs Higgins dropped the sugar mice into her enormous shopping basket on wheels, where a dark paw reached out to claim them. She pinched Lottie's cheek as she left and murmured something about the poor motherless dear, which usually would have had Lottie fuming, but right now she just didn't care.

"Don't ever drink her 'tea', Lottie," Uncle Jack warned. "Lethal stuff. Turns your wee blue," he added in a whisper.

Lottie blinked at him and he stared at her in concern. "Not even a tiny giggle? What's up,

Lottie?" Then his face hardened. "It's her, isn't it? Pandora. What's she done now? She didn't try and get in your head again? Did Ariadne's spells work?"

Lottie shook her head. "She's cleverer than that. She went for Ruby instead. Ruby's hardly talking to me and she wanted to go in Pandora's shop. She's bought this evil little black toy cat. I don't know what to do. It's almost like she can't see me. She's not going to listen if I try to tell her what Pandora really is."

Uncle Jack frowned and Sofie nuzzled Lottie's ankles comfortingly. "Ruby will come round," she said, her voice only slightly doubtful. "Pandora will not deceive her for long."

Lottie looked down at her. "No, you don't understand. Pandora's bewitched her, Sofie, she must have done."

"It does sound like it." Uncle Jack sighed.

"What can we do?" Lottie asked. "How do you break a spell?"

"It is not easy." Sofie shook her ears. "Not easy at all."

"You need some idea of how it's been cast," Uncle Jack explained. "Pandora probably discovered Ruby when she was in your mind the other night."

"She hinted something like that," Lottie admitted. "I'm pretty sure she got Ruby to touch a doll from her shop. Zara had it at school. The thing is, Ruby didn't start being odd until today. She was just like herself yesterday, even after she'd touched the doll. So I don't think that was the whole spell. Maybe Pandora was just using it to get a feel for Ruby? Does that make sense? To find her so she could do the spell? I've no idea how she actually cast it, though. How do I find something like that out?"

Sofie and Uncle Jack exchanged glances and Sofie shrugged expressively. "You cannot. Unless you go into her mind."

Lottie glared at them. "Are you mad? Is that the best suggestion you've got?

She'd mince me!"

"You underestimate yourself, Lottie, always," Sofie told her quietly.

"No point in sending untrained troops into battle," a squeaky voice pointed out from the wobbling mound of straw bedding in Giles's cage. He was back to sleeping in the shop now that Lottie had learned the guarding spells to ward off Pandora while she was asleep. Eventually he lumbered out of his nest and came towards the cage bars. "Lottie has the talent, to be sure, but she needs training! Drills! Discipline!"

"You sound just like Ariadne," Lottie sighed.

Giles marched up and down his cage lecturing them like a commanding officer. "To meet the enemy, one must be prepared! Mentally! Physically! Psychologologogically!" He paused there, and coughed, as though he suspected he might have got that slightly wrong. "Emotionally, as well," he added, combing his whiskers with an embarrassed paw.

"Because one day I think Lottie will have to fight her." Sofie's ears drooped. Evidently she was as worried about this as Lottie was.

The tense silence was broken by the clang of the shop bell and the door swung slowly open.

"What the. . ." Uncle Jack peered round. The door seemed to have opened by itself. Little scratchy, scurrying footsteps pattered in and everyone looked at the floor.

Staring up at them were two large and beautiful blue lizards, both looking rather bluer than usual. Lottie gazed down at them in surprise – they were unmistakable. Ruby's pets, Sam and Joe.

"For pity's sake, a fan heater," Joe gasped.

"Hair dryer, hot water bottle, anything!" Sam added. "It's icy out there!"

Lottie gave them a surprised look. It was a nice, crisp October day now, not particularly cold. But then Sam and Joe were cold-blooded and lived in a heated tank in Ruby's bedroom. Probably it did feel freezing to them.

Uncle Jack was fussing around, boiling the kettle, and trying to remember where Grandma Maisie's old electric blanket was, while the lizards shivered and grumbled.

"Above and beyond the call of duty, Lottie, that's what this is," Sam growled.

"Duty has no higher limit," Giles pronounced disapprovingly.

Sam and Joe turned their disconcerting reptilian glare on him, but he didn't seem to mind. All the mice had hidden themselves under their bedding – they hated lizards. But Giles merely stared back, looking unimpressed. "To do one's duty is the highest calling of any creature," Giles said loftily. "Even reptiles," he added.

Uncle Jack reappeared with two hot water bottles and the lizards surged on to them with moans of relief. "Aaahhh, that's better. My scales felt like they were falling off," Sam said gratefully. "What is that creature over there?" he asked Uncle Jack quietly as he put a blanket over his tail.

"A hamster," Uncle Jack explained.

"Ah. Fierce?"

"Extremely."

"Um-hm." Sam gave Giles a thoughtful look. "Quite small. No more than a few mouthfuls."

"Large teeth though," Joe muttered. "Crazy eyes, too, if you ask me."

"Why are you two here?" Lottie asked, thinking it might be a good time to interrupt.

Sam and Joe exchanged a worried glance. "It's Ruby," Sam explained.

Joe leaned forward and hissed impressively, "She forgot to feed us!"

"She's *never* done that before," Sam said sorrowfully.

"Oh my goodness, I'll get you some food at once." Uncle Jack was horrified. He adored lizards and Sam and Joe were particularly rare and interesting. They were, according to them anyway, dragons. But Lottie wasn't sure if that was just wishful thinking. Their one aim was to breathe fire and they were convinced they would do it one day.

Uncle Jack found a sack of his homemade lizard treats, squashy black lumps that were made out of mashed-up things Lottie didn't want to know about. But they did at least mean the pet shop never had any spiders. Sam and Joe gorged themselves, managing three each before they collapsed on the counter, burping gently.

"Is that better?" Uncle Jack asked anxiously. "You must have been starving."

Sam smiled sleepily at him. "Well, no. Ruby didn't feed us, but we're quite capable of opening the food box."

"But it was very nice of you to worry," Joe told him kindly.

Uncle Jack made a face and moved the rest of the treats out of reach. "Just don't be sick!"

Sam gave one last enormous burp and sat up, looking business-like. "What's important is that Ruby is not herself."

"Definitely not," Joe agreed. "She's hardly looked at us the last couple of days."

"Except that odd moment last night," Sam put in. "She was dreaming, I think. Wriggling about in her sleep. Then she got up and came and stood, leaning against the glass of our tank. Her face was white and her eyes were strange. She was still asleep, maybe. She stood there for ages, muttering, saying that she didn't understand and she couldn't think."

"She's been bewitched." Joe nodded importantly. "We need you to rescue her."

Lottie nodded. "Yes, we think the same. But we don't know how to break the spell. You two could look for clues, though, couldn't you? Something to tell us how Pandora cast the spell in the first place."

"Pandora? You mean you know who did it?" Sam looked up at her sharply.

Lottie hung her head, feeling ashamed that she was letting her friend down. "Yes, but it doesn't help. We don't know how to stop her."

Sam and Joe stared at her, their round black eyes hard. Eventually they seemed to decide she was telling the truth. "We'll go back and look," they agreed. "We'll watch her. She may let something slip."

"How did you get here, though?" Lottie asked suddenly.

"We walked," Joe said bitterly.

"And no one saw you?" Uncle Jack asked in surprise. "You were lucky."

"I'll carry you back in my rucksack," Lottie suggested. "Uncle Jack, is there any way Sam and Joe can let us know if they find a clue without having to come back again?"

"If you let us, we can speak in your thoughts," Sam suggested. "We would have done that this time but you've got a thick wall up."

"Oh!" Lottie hadn't realized that the lizards could talk telepathically. "Usually only Sofie does that. And Tabitha and Shadow, I suppose." The unicorn had spoken in her mind too, but as that night was becoming only a memory, Lottie was slowly beginning to wonder if she'd imagined him after all.

Uncle Jack smiled. "Most creatures can if you let them, Lottie. But at the moment, I think you're wise to be cautious. Just let your guard down for a minute, so Sam and Joe can feel your mind."

It was hard to relax the defences she had built up so carefully. Lottie closed her eyes and stilled her breathing, seeking out the lizards. She'd never felt for them before and their minds were slow and different and strange.

We'll find you again, Lottie.

Yes, we'll find you when we need you, Sam told her approvingly. *Good girl.*

Lottie blinked, and then opened her eyes. It felt odd looking at the bright paint of the shop and the glittering metal of the cages. Even the lizards' blue scales seemed glaring. Their thoughts had been quiet and softly tinted, and the rest of the world seemed too loud.

"I'll take you back home," she said, tipping her books out of her rucksack. "Sofie, do you want a walk?"

Sofie uncurled herself luxuriously. "Not really, but I will come. You do not want Ruby to see you out near her house without an excuse."

Lottie flushed slightly. Of course, Sofie knew what she was thinking, but she did sometimes wish that the little dachshund wouldn't *tell* everybody.

"Lottie, wake up! The sun is shining. I want to go out!"

Lottie groaned. Sofie was rarely energetic, but she could be an unstoppable force when she felt like it. She adored the sun and she'd missed it these last few misty days.

"We must go to the park!" Sofie said, stomping her front paws up and down on Lottie's stomach so there was absolutely no chance of her going back to sleep.

"Now?" Lottie asked feebly. "On a Saturday? Before breakfast?"

"Oh, well, no. . ." Sofie jumped off the bed. "Of course not before breakfast. I will have a croissant. Come *on*, Lottie!"

Lottie staggered out of bed and got dressed, then headed downstairs to find Sofie already sipping delicately at a bowl of black coffee. Uncle Jack was warming croissants. Lottie poured herself some orange juice and tried to stay awake. She'd dreamed about Pandora's shop all night, it felt like, seeing odd, mean little faces peeping out at her from the glass ornaments. The worst thing was, she'd seen Ruby too, reflected in them. And she was screaming.

Lottie shuddered and pushed away her juice. She couldn't taste it properly anyway.

"Walk!" Sofie said briskly, watching her. "You will feel better. I shall fetch my lead."

Sofie was right. It was a gorgeous autumn day and Lottie did feel better watching Sofie jumping through the piles of orangey-brown leaves gathered by the side of the road. She sank into them almost to chin height and bounded along, ears flapping madly.

"Was that extra-strong coffee?" Lottie muttered, but Sofie just shook her ears happily.

They weren't the only ones in the park. Lots of people from Lottie's school were hanging about, the boys mostly throwing leaves at each other, or playing football. It was one of the things that Lottie loved about Netherbridge – the town was so quiet and safe that parents let their children do far more things on their own than she'd ever been allowed to at home.

"Look, Zara!" The fur along Sofie's spine was sticking up a little and her ears were pricked watchfully. Lottie glanced over, trying to be casual. She still didn't want to get into anything with Zara, even if she wasn't as scared of her as she used to be.

Zara's little gang was sitting round the edge of the marble fountain, which had been turned off at the end of the summer. They were gossiping and giggling, and Zara's chief confidante, Bethany, had just pointed Lottie out.

"Ignore them," Sofie said, prancing on and jumping at a falling leaf. "Look, Danny is over there, playing football. And there is Ruby too, under that tree."

Lottie caught her breath anxiously. She'd almost called Ruby this morning, after all those horrible dreams, but Ruby's strange behaviour the day before had put her off. What if Ruby wouldn't talk to her? Lottie couldn't bear to hear her best friend tell her to go away. Ruby had helped her to settle in in Netherbridge. Lottie needed her. And she was pretty sure that Ruby needed her too, especially now.

Telling herself not to be so silly and that maybe Ruby had just been having a bad day, Lottie strolled over to her. "Hey!" she said, a little hesitantly. "Are you OK?"

She'd been hoping that Ruby would be back to her old self, full of their plans for tonight – their Halloween night in with popcorn and a girlie film with strictly no monsters, ghosts or evil twins. But Ruby looked up at her blankly and Lottie's heart sank. She was the same as before, or maybe worse. It was as though she wasn't sure who Lottie was. She smiled politely but her face brightened as she saw Sofie. She crouched down to stroke her ears.

Sofie looked up at Lottie thoughtfully. Lottie shrugged. She knew what Sofie was asking – whether she could talk to Ruby now? She had before, of course, but now they weren't sure whose side Ruby was on, or how she'd react to a talking dog. In the middle of a park full of people wasn't the time to find out.

But it seemed that stroking Sofie was bringing Ruby back to her senses. Perhaps Sofie's magic, which was so linked to Lottie's, was working against Pandora's spell. Ruby stopped petting Sofie's ears and looked at her in confusion. "What *are* you?" she murmured, drawing her hand back and staring at it.

Sofie opened her big dark eyes wide and fluttered her eyelashes, trying to look as innocent as possible. She overdid it slightly.

Ruby stood up, blinking, and backed away, glaring suspiciously at Lottie. "Are you making fun of me?" she asked angrily. "Teaching your dog to do tricks – it's . . . it's not nice!"

Lottie caught her breath, not sure what to say. She obviously couldn't tell Ruby that she hadn't taught Sofie anything, that in fact it was the other way around. "She didn't mean to. . ." Lottie muttered, knowing it sounded stupid.

"I hate you!" Ruby snapped, her blue eyes sparkling furiously and her dark-red curls escaping from under her hat like angry snakes.

It was no comfort to Lottie to know that this was all due to Pandora's spell. Tears burned at the back of her eyes. "You don't! No, you don't!" she whispered miserably.

"Ooh, look! Lottie and Ruby are having a little fight!" someone jeered, and Lottie spun round in horror. Zara, of course. She'd forgotten that the gang were there by the fountain. They had an amazing nose for trouble.

"Lottie's *crying*. . ." Bethany laughed.

Lottie sniffed defiantly. "No, I'm not," she snapped. "And it's none of your business what Ruby and I are talking about, Bethany. Get lost."

"Does *Ruby* want us to get lost?" Zara asked silkily. She was an expert at divide and rule. "Maybe you're being mean to her. I'm not sure we should leave her alone with you. Especially not with that vicious little dog around."

"You're more vicious than she is!" Lottie cried. "Ruby, I know you're upset with me, but this is *Zara*! Come on! Tell her to leave us alone. Please!"

Ruby was turning her head from side to side, looking confused and angry. "Why don't *you* leave me alone, Lottie," she snapped. "Don't boss me around. I'll talk to who I want, and right now I don't want to talk to you!"

"Go Ruby, go Ruby!" Zara and her mates chanted, like cheerleaders egging them on.

Ruby smiled slightly. She still looked confused, but it was obviously easier to accept Zara's support than work out what was going on here. She stepped up closer to Lottie, and hissed, "Just get lost!"

It was a mistake to come so close. Lottie's misery boiled over into anger and she snapped back. "Fine! Go off and play with your new *friends* if you've forgotten what they're really like! I just hope you don't regret it, that's all!"

Sofie growled angrily and Ruby hissed at her too. "Horrible little dog! I could step on you!"

Lottie and Sofie lost their temper together. Lottie shoved Ruby and Sofie bit her. It wasn't a very hard bite as she had to make a flying leap to get above Ruby's red leather boots, but she tore Ruby's tights just below the knee and her teeth grazed the skin. Half triumphant, half shocked at what they'd done, Lottie scooped Sofie up protectively in case Ruby should try anything.

She didn't. She stood there, looking down at the slowly bleeding scratch, as though she didn't know how she'd got it. She didn't even say anything. It was left for Zara and the others to screech about vicious dogs and calling the police.

At last Ruby looked up and stared Lottie right in the face. She didn't seem confused any more. She was frightened and Lottie had an awful feeling that she was frightened of herself. Ruby's blue eyes held hers with a pleading expression. She was begging.

"Lottie – help me!"

Chapter 6

Zara had hustled Ruby away but Lottie hadn't tried to stop them. The mist had closed down over Ruby's eyes again after she'd begged for help. It seemed that the pain of Sofie's bite had jolted her out of the spell for just long enough. Now it had swallowed her up again.

Lottie started to trudge home carrying Sofie. At least she now knew for certain that Ruby was under a spell, and it wasn't just that her friend didn't like her any more. But she'd been pretty sure about that anyway, except in her most doubtful moments. What she still didn't know was what on earth she was going to do about it.

Running footsteps thudding over the grass behind her made her turn quickly, thinking that it might be Zara and the others. She sighed gratefully when she realized it was only Danny.

"What happened?" he gasped. "I was on the other side of the field and I couldn't see properly. Jake said he saw Sofie bite Ruby!"

"I was provoked," Sofie muttered sulkily.

"You didn't?" Danny asked in dismay.

"I might have done. . ." Sofie spoke to the air over Lottie's shoulder so as not to look at Danny. She knew quite well that biting wasn't allowed.

"She did. But Ruby was being really mean. And it was a good thing," Lottie promised him. "It brought Ruby out of the spell for a minute. She asked us to help her."

"Anyway, Lottie pushed her first," Sofie added.

"Wow," Danny muttered. "I wish I'd been there now."

"You don't," Lottie said sadly. "It was horrible. She was being so nasty and then when she asked us for help, she just looked really confused. Like she didn't know what was going on inside her." She sniffed. "You won't tell your dad, will you?"

Danny glared at her. "Oh yes, because I'm going to go straight home and say, *Da–ad, Lottie shoved her frie–ennnnd.* Honestly, Lottie, what do you think I am? A girl?"

"I'll shove you next," Lottie muttered. But he did cheer her up a bit.

"There has to be a way of breaking Ruby out of that spell for good," Danny said thoughtfully as they turned into their road. "Hey, cross over, Lottie. I'm not walking past that shop, it gives me the creeps."

Lottie gave him a surprised look.

"What? It's horrible!" exclaimed Danny. "Have you been making yourself walk right past the windows?"

"I went *in* it with Ruby," Lottie admitted.

"You're mad. There's no point in giving her a golden opportunity to mess with your head twice a day, Lottie. Those windows are really strong. Pick your battles. Hey, that reminds me. We'll get Giles and ask him to help us break the spell. Sep's been talking to him and he says he's got some great ideas."

"He was amazing when Pandora came to the shop," Lottie agreed. "He wasn't scared of her at all."

"I did tell you he was also utterly mad," Septimus's head popped out from the pocket of Danny's fleece. "There's brave and then there's just stupid."

They woke Giles by all standing in front of his cage and coughing loudly, and he gladly agreed to go up to Lottie's room for what he called a tactical planning session.

"Situation's becoming a bit desperate, what?" he squeaked, marching up and down Lottie's duvet. "Time to put on our thinking caps, men! And ladies, of course, so sorry." He bowed to Lottie and Sofie. Sofie sniffed.

"When dealing with enemy whose forces are superior – and I mean that only in terms of her experience, dear Lottie – one must resort to underhand tactics." Giles nodded happily to himself.

"She's done that already though, by getting at Ruby," Lottie pointed out.

"Espionage. That's what we need," Giles told them firmly. "A spy network."

"Ruby's lizards are watching her for any clues," Lottie told him hopefully. "You mean like that?"

"Excellent, Lottie! You have the makings of an officer!" Giles gave her an approving nod. "Although, lizards, you know. Not the most reliable chaps. Always go for a rodent if you can, Lottie. Someone like Septimus here, or that splendid little lad, Fred. The pink one. So. When did the lizard squad last report in?"

"Er. . . They haven't yet," Lottie admitted, feeling rather silly.

"Reptiles," Giles muttered irritably. "No sense of duty. Call them up, Lottie dear. Demand a status report!"

"How do I do that?" Lottie muttered to Sofie, trying not to look stupid in front of Danny and the others.

Try and think lizard, Sofie told her. *Slow your mind down. Enjoy the sunshine.*

Hey, it's Lottie!

Lottie jumped. That had been easier than she thought. *Hi Joe. Hi Sam.*

Lottie, we were just about to try and call you. We think we've got something. Oddly, the lizards seemed to speak together. Lottie wondered if it was to give their voices the strength to cross the distance.

"They've got something for us!" Lottie told the others excitedly.

Ruby's mother keeps wandering round the house looking for a sketchbook. She asked Ruby if she'd borrowed it, but Ruby said no. Her mum's upset because there was loads of stuff in it, work for a big painting she's about to start. And there was a drawing of Ruby too, that she wanted to frame and give to Ruby's dad for Christmas. We've looked too,

Lottie, and that book isn't anywhere. Someone's taken it.

"Would Pandora be able to use a drawing of Ruby to cast the spell?" Lottie asked Sofie and the others. "One of Ruby's mum's sketchbooks has disappeared." She shuddered. "Ugh, that means she's been in Ruby's house."

She won't be back again, the lizards told her. *We'll make sure of that. But do you think that could be it?*

"Yes," Sofie agreed. She could hear Joe and Sam too. "It must be that, Lottie. Tell them to keep watching though."

Lottie nodded, and said goodbye to the lizards.

"Hey, wait a minute," Danny interrupted her. "Lottie, ask Sam and Joe if there was anything special about that drawing. You never know." He shrugged.

We heard, Sam and Joe told her before she could ask. *It was in pastels. Soft colours. Very good. It looked just like her. She had those hair bobbles in, the ones you gave her from Paris. That was why Ruby's mother wanted to frame it, because it was just like her. You could feel her in it, more than a photograph. Goodbye, Lottie. We'll keep watch, don't worry.* And they were gone.

"A pastel drawing," Danny said thoughtfully. "Would that work?"

"Could you hear what the lizards were saying too, then?" Lottie asked in surprise.

Danny blinked. "Um, yes. We all could. When you started talking again, when I asked if there was something special about the drawing. We could hear Sam and Joe when they answered you. It just seemed to work like that. I didn't notice we were doing it. They heard me, too, didn't they?" he added thoughtfully.

Lottie nodded slowly. "We ought to be careful. If you can hear me when I'm talking to Sam and Joe, who else can? Do you have all those mind guard things, like Ariadne taught me? If Pandora wants to get at us, she might try you too."

Danny stared at her seriously. "She's tried, Lottie."

"You didn't tell me! Are you OK?" Lottie gave him a worried look.

"I'm not under a spell if that's what you're thinking. Dad told me stuff to do, after Pandora twisted your dreams." He grinned. "I recite football scores at her. Works really well – I can feel her getting cross. And I guess us being cousins makes it easier for us to see into each other's minds – I don't think anyone else could break in."

"OK." Lottie nodded. "I suppose so."

Sofie nudged her reassuringly. "Do not worry, Lottie. Pandora does not have the gift with animals that you and Danny share. Her dogs did what she said because they were scared. Not for love. She would not be able to read *our* minds."

Lottie hugged her. *I can't imagine doing this without you,* she told Sofie silently. "So," she added out loud. "Do you think she did steal the drawing? Would that work?"

Giles nodded. "Think about it. A drawing that not only looks like this girl, it has the *feel* of her too. And drawn by her mother. It's full of power."

Lottie nodded. "You know, I've just remembered, I've seen that drawing. Ruby's mum showed me it because Ruby had those green bobbles in her hair, the ones I got Mum to send. She thought I'd like to see it." Lottie thought carefully for a minute, remembering the sketchbook, then let the others share her memory of the drawing.

"Very like her." Sofie nodded. "Dangerous."

"Do you think her hair makes a difference?" Danny asked, sounding a little embarrassed, as though he thought this was a bit of a girly thing to say.

Everyone stared at him and he blushed. "Well, you know. Those bobble things. If Pandora cast the spell using a picture of Ruby wearing them, with her hair up, does the spell still work if she's got her hair down?"

"Oh!" Lottie tried to think back. "She had those bobbles in on Friday when she started being weird! Maybe it makes the spell stronger if she looks like the picture."

Giles suddenly stood up on Lottie's bed, looking excited. "She needs the drawing!" he exclaimed. "She wouldn't have bothered to steal it if she didn't, would she? She's left herself open by taking it – we've discovered what she did. She could have just borrowed it. So she must need to have it to keep the spell working." He stared round at them all triumphantly. "So all we have to do is steal it back."

Everyone stared back, not wanting to say it. Finally, Danny muttered, "Oh, so that's all. . . No problem then."

Giles looked at them all, a madly excited glitter in his little black eyes. "Come on, cheer up! We have a plan. This is excellent."

"Giles, our plan is stealing from an enchantress," Lottie wailed. "It isn't excellent, it's scary!"

"But Lottie, until now we didn't have a plan at all," Giles told her gently, as though speaking to a very small child. "This is a huge step forward."

"Can we step back?" Lottie pleaded. "This isn't a plan, it's a death wish."

"And we know where she lives," Giles pointed out happily. "So we have a plan *and* a location. This is most satisfactory." He actually rubbed his paws together in delight.

"We can't break into her house!" Lottie said in a horrified whisper.

"We could both go into the shop and one of us distract her somehow," Danny suggested.

"She is evil, Danny, not stupid," Sofie put in disgustedly.

"We can't just give up," Danny protested. Lottie looked at him nervously. He seemed to have been infected with Giles's enthusiasm and his eyes had a little of that same mad glitter.

"There is one time that we could do it," Sofie said slowly, and the others stared at her. She looked up at Lottie and continued reluctantly. "Tonight."

"Tonight?" Lottie squeaked. "Why? Oh! You mean Halloween. . ."

"She will be out, on the hills, I am sure," Sofie went on reluctantly. "When we saw her in your dream, that was the place she chose. And she would choose a place where she is powerful to attack you. On Halloween she will be there – in her place of strength. Not in that strange little shop."

Danny nodded. "Sofie's right. Most people like to be outside on Halloween, anyway. Our sort, I mean."

"I don't," Lottie said miserably. She didn't want to think about scary Halloween rituals. She'd been looking forward to that popcorn. "And what if we're wrong and she hasn't gone out? Or it starts raining and she comes back?"

"You are being very feeble, Lottie," Giles told her disapprovingly.

"I'm only being sensible!" Lottie complained.

"Where is your sense of adventure?" demanded Giles, starting to march up and down her bed again. "Your spirit of derring-do?"

"My what?" Lottie muttered.

"Too much association with reptiles," Giles told Septimus quietly, or at least he thought he was being quiet. "Not a good influence."

"If you want, I'll follow her, Lottie," Danny suggested. Lottie looked up at him in surprise and he shrugged. "Well, you've got Sofie and Giles to help you search the shop, you won't need me. I bet you could get the pink mice to help too. If we watch the shop, I can go after her when she leaves and warn you when she looks like she's coming back."

Lottie nodded. It was a good plan. It was the only plan they had. And she was going to have to go through with it for Ruby's sake, however much she hated the idea. She was going to burgle a witch's house, on Halloween.

Chapter 7

"Where does Uncle Jack keep the rose-hip brandy?" Lottie asked, searching through the drawers of the counter.

"What do you want that for?" Danny asked from the doorway where he was keeping watch through a crack of the door. "Still no sign of her."

"I need to bribe Fred and Peach and the others. I can't search a whole house by myself, and I know they're only tiny but there are lots of them. They can help me look. That lot will do anything for mouse brandy."

"You're going to take a troop of drunken mice on a top-secret mission?" Danny said doubtfully.

"No! I'm only going to show them the bottle. They can have the brandy when we get back.

Oh, here it is!" Lottie pulled out a little brown glass bottle from the back of a drawer and clinked it meaningfully on the counter.

There was a sudden hush as the background noise of scuffling and squeaking that always filled the shop died away. In every cage heads appeared with twitching whiskers. And on the top shelf, the seven pink mice stopped playing I Spy (they were fighting because Fred had kept them guessing for ten minutes for something beginning with K and he was refusing to believe that "cat" didn't). They practically vaulted out of their cage and stood in a line on their shelf, staring down at Lottie.

"Would that be your uncle's private stash of brandy, by any chance?" Fred asked casually, but he was wringing his tail in his paws with excitement.

Lottie pulled the stopper out of the bottle and a waft of pink smoke coiled upwards. Every mouse in the shop, and Septimus and

Giles, breathed in ecstatically.

"Oh my flourishing whiskers!" Giles muttered. "That's strong stuff."

Lottie jammed the stopper back in.

"Lottie!" protested Peach, Fred's partner in crime. "That's torture. You can't do that! It's cruelty to dumb animals."

"Um, Peach. . . We aren't dumb animals. We can talk," Fred hissed.

"Ssshhh! She doesn't need to know that!" Peach hissed back.

"Er, excuse me?" Lottie broke in politely. "Anyone who wants *a whole thimbleful of mouse brandy* can have it later on, if they come out with me tonight."

"A whole thimbleful?" Fred whispered gleefully.

"They'll be dead after a whole thimbleful!" Danny called from the door.

Lottie had seen the effects of Uncle Jack's powerful brew, so she was pretty sure the mice would all be asleep after three sips, but she shrugged. "I'm sure they're all mouse enough to take the risk."

The pink mice were already climbing down the shelves eagerly, but the others were less foolhardy. "Where would we have to go?" a pretty, pink-eyed, white mouse called from her cage.

Lottie eyed the pink mice anxiously and tried to sound casual. "Just down the road." She paused. "To Pandora's shop."

"Where?" the little white mouse squealed. "Are you mad? Not for a whole bottle!" And she dived into her bedding and curled up in a quivering ball with her tail wrapped round her ears.

The rest of the mice slunk to the back of their cages and pretended they hadn't heard what Lottie said in the first place. There was a sudden clattering of exercise wheels as they all tried to find something to do. But the pink mice, Lottie's favourites, were trooping across the floor and scurrying up her leg to the counter. They formed a worshipful ring around the brandy bottle.

"Are you coming then?" Lottie asked hopefully.

"Of course!" Fred told her. "But Lottie, we do have one very important question. . ."

Lottie nodded. "I know. It *is* going to be risky. I can't deny it. But I promise I'll do my best to keep us all safe."

Fred blinked at her and waved a paw dismissively. "No, no, no. Lottie, listen." He stared up at her and all the others watched them anxiously. "Are we talking about a big thimble or a small one?"

"She's gone!" Danny hissed, and Lottie crept over to the door. They were alone in the shop, apart from the animals. Uncle Jack had gone out an hour before looking oddly preoccupied. Lottie was feeling even more uneasy about Halloween now. It didn't feel like a special night to her and she couldn't help worrying in case that meant she was useless at magic. But then, Danny didn't seem too bothered about it either. Maybe she just had to be older?

It was velvety dark outside, as all the street lamps seemed to have fizzled and faded to nothing. Swirls of mist were coiling along the pavement, but overhead the moon shone high and clear and bright.

A tall figure was moving swiftly down the road, a dark coat wrapped tightly round it.

"Are you sure that's her?" Lottie whispered.

"She came out of the shop. And anyway, look at the hair. She's got the dogs with her too – they're running ahead." Danny pointed out two shadowy shapes floating through the mist further up the street.

"Oh, yes, you're right," Lottie murmured as she saw Pandora flick back her long curtain of white-blonde hair.

"Right. I'll get after her." Danny prepared to slide stealthily out of the doorway, but Lottie grabbed his sleeve. "Don't!"

"Lottie! I have to – that's what we planned. Let go, I'll lose her." Danny peered anxiously out again.

"But we don't know what she's going out to do. Something horrible, probably! What if she catches you spying on her? Danny. . ." Lottie gulped. "She might even kill you!"

"Look, I'm not going to get that close to her. I just need to make sure she's still out there and not coming back to the shop. Besides, Lottie, if anything goes wrong, you'll be able to tell, I'm sure you will. Like I could hear you talking to Sam and Joe earlier. Cousins. We're linked, if we want to be." He shot her a fleeting glimpse of himself, looking stubborn. "You can come and help me."

Lottie let go reluctantly. "Just don't do anything stupid," she warned him.

Danny grinned. "I promise." And he slid out into the night, running soft-footed down the road.

Lottie turned back into the shop to find Giles and the mice lined up on the counter, even the usually silly mice looking almost military. Sofie was perched on the stool behind them, an anxious look in her dark eyes.

"Ready, men?" Giles demanded, and the mice immediately started to twitter and fuss. "Silence! This is a covert mission which must be undertaken with the most extreme discretion!"

The mice all nodded obediently, but the smallest one at the back turned round and muttered to Sofie, "What does that mean?"

Sofie leaned close. "It means *shut up*."

The mouse looked much reassured. "I thought it did. I just wanted to check. Are we going now?"

Giles gave Lottie a long-suffering look. "All present and correct!" he reported, sticking his chest out proudly. Lottie thought he would probably have saluted if his paws were long enough.

"OK." Lottie picked up her little rucksack. It had lots of pockets and Giles and the mice climbed in, peeping out over the top. Sofie jumped down from the stool and went to wait by the door. Everyone was quiet and tense, even the mice.

Her heart thudding most uncomfortably, Lottie walked the few metres down the street to Pandora's shop. She had tried to find spells about keys and locks in one of the books Ariadne had lent her, but she hadn't come up with anything useful. However the mice assured her that she had no need to worry. They would be able to get in with no problem and they would open the door for her and Sofie and Giles. Or, "you fat ones", as they put it.

Outside the shop, Lottie lurked in a side alley while the mice scurried out of her pockets and swarmed up a drain pipe. Lottie could just make them out as they flitted across a low bit of roof. Pandora's shop was built in a similar way to Uncle Jack's, all mixed up and squashed together, as though everyone who'd lived there had thought it too small and added another room. It made it a bit worrying in a high wind. The mice were making for a window that had been left slightly open, and Lottie clapped her hands silently as she saw seven pink tails disappear inside one after the other.

A couple of minutes later the door swung open eerily and a little pink head poked out of the letterbox. "Hurry up!" squeaked Fred. "This place is horrible."

Lottie had hated the shop yesterday in the daytime; at night it was a place out of the worst kind of nightmare. Painted faces leered at them out of the darkness. Lottie closed the door behind them with a dull thud and clicked on her torch, dreading what she might see in its light.

A collection of stuffed toys stared back at her with huge glass eyes glowing red in the torchlight. Lottie was sure they twitched as she swept the torch over them. She turned the torch on the counter, but no picture of Ruby was lying on it, as she'd secretly hoped. They would have to go further in.

"This place has a very bad smell," Sofie whispered.

"I can only smell those horrible incense sticks," Lottie whispered back. "Can you smell something else?"

Sofie took another cautious sniff. "Bad spells make bad smells," she muttered. "Let us start looking. I want not to be here."

Lottie nodded. "I don't think she would keep it down here," she said thoughtfully. "Although I wouldn't put it past her to frame it and keep it in the shop. . . No, I think it will be hidden upstairs, or wherever she has her workroom." She stepped bravely towards the door behind the counter, trying to keep the torch pointing only towards the door and nothing else, but she still couldn't help catching glimpses of odd things as they passed. The china figures whispered in tiny cracked voices and Lottie had a sudden, horrible thought. What if Pandora had set spies to watch too, like Lottie and Danny? What if all these figures, the bears, the puppets and everything else, could speak to her? What if they were calling her back right now, warning her about an invader? Perhaps Pandora was walking down the street, leaving Danny collapsed on the hillside, about to corner Lottie in the dark?

Lottie took a deep, steadying breath, feeling the comforting warmth of the mice and Giles all huddling against her neck, their tiny paws wound in her hair.

"Danny will not fail you," Sofie told her, looking back as she approached the door. "If the enchantress is coming back, he *will* tell us."

"I know. I think I just panicked for a moment," Lottie admitted. "This place gives me the creeps.

"It's meant to," Giles pointed out. "The best generals fight with their minds, Lottie. Those toys are all just paint and clay, remember."

Paint and clay and a lot of terrible magic, Lottie thought to herself. But she nodded and they headed up the narrow stairway. Pandora seemed to have spent most of her time organizing and bewitching the shop and the upper floor was very bare. It made Pandora seem less human, somehow, that she didn't even seem to want cushions or a picture on the wall. Not even a postcard from a friend. Nothing.

"Perhaps it'll be easy to search," Lottie said hopefully. "There's hardly anything here."

But even the barest house still takes a lot of searching and it was a good half an hour later that Lottie sat back on her heels in front of a battered old trunk in the living room and sighed. "I really thought it would have to be in here," she told Sofie. "The kitchen's just like any other kitchen, there's nothing in the bathroom, and only a bed and a wardrobe in the bedroom. I don't know where she does all her spells because I haven't found anything that looks magical, except these books in here." She shut the lid of the trunk gratefully. The books were all bound in dark leather and smelled of must. They were cold too, Lottie was sure. Cold seemed to be seeping out of them into the air.

"I should think she does them in her head," Sofie said, scuffling down the back of the armchair. "No, there is nothing. What do we do now?"

Lottie looked round anxiously. "Try the bedroom again? Perhaps we missed something in the wardrobe. I thought I did look through all those shoeboxes, but I might have lost count."

"You did not lose count." Sofie shook her head. "They were all just shoes. I think she has it with her, this picture."

"Lottie!"

Something sharp in Fred's squeak brought Lottie to her feet at once. "What is it?"

The mice were gathered by another pile of books, large ones, and they'd pulled one of them off the top of the pile. Lottie had skimmed through them earlier, but not found anything that looked like a drawing.

"Oh, yes, her photograph album. We're looking for a drawing though, not a photo. Sorry, Fred."

"Lottie, look at the photo." Fred's voice sounded more serious than she had ever heard him, so Lottie looked, even though she didn't want to. Why would she want to see photos of Pandora? It was hateful enough being in her house. She crouched down next to the mice who were standing on the album and Sofie nosed her way in too. They all stared down at the photograph.

At last Giles cleared his throat. "Ahem! That looks rather like your uncle, Lottie."

Lottie shook her head. "No." Her voice was

very quiet. "It isn't my uncle. It's my father."

"With Pandora," Sofie whispered, and Lottie nodded.

They were a couple, it was easy to see. Lottie's dad had his arm round her and she was looking up at him. They looked so happy.

"They're very young," Fred said comfortingly. "It must have been a long time ago, Lottie."

"Why didn't anyone tell me?" Lottie muttered. "Are there any more pictures of them?"

The mice turned through the pages finding several more photos of Lottie's dad. There they were sitting by the fountain in the park and there leaning against the parapet of the bridge over the river.

"They were here," Lottie said blankly. "These were all taken round here."

"She said that she had lived here before," Sofie reminded her.

"Take it out," Lottie said to Fred. "That first

one. Pull it out of the album."

"If you do that, Lottie, she'll know we've been here," Giles warned her.

"She'll know anyway." Lottie looked around the bare, miserable little room. "She'll know. She'll be able to feel me. She'll feel how angry I am. Come on. We're going to Ariadne's. I want to know what really happened and Uncle Jack won't tell me. I'm not going to let them sweet-talk me again."

Lottie hammered on the door of Ariadne's flat, impatient and angry. Catching her mood, Sofie scrabbled anxiously at the door with her paws.

It didn't open.

"I suppose we should have expected they'd be out tonight," Lottie said, the anger suddenly disappearing, leaving her limp and tired. She sat down on the stairs, her eyes filling with weary tears.

Sofie, Giles and the mice swarmed into her

lap, Sofie gently licking away Lottie's tears and the mice crooning comfort and compliments as they scurried round her shoulders. Giles climbed to the top of her rucksack and perched there, trying to jolly her along.

"Very difficult situation to be in, Lottie, old thing. Worrying." Seeing that it wasn't working, he dropped the bluff, cheerful voice for a moment and looked her straight in the eye. "Just remember, Lottie. It's *you* that matters. Your choices, what you do. Not what your parents did before you were even thought of."

Lottie sniffed and nodded. "I know. But I still want to understand. I mean . . . how could he?" She leaned her head against the wall and closed her eyes. The photograph was in one of the pockets of her rucksack but she didn't need to see it. She felt as though it was burned on to her brain. The way they looked at each other. Could she remember her parents ever looking at each other like that?

"Are we staying here, Lottie?" Sofie

asked gently.

Lottie nodded, not speaking. Then she murmured, "Sorry. You can go back to the shop if you're tired. I want to wait for Ariadne."

"Do not be so foolish," Sofie told her sternly. "We are not leaving you. But we ought to tell Danny that he can go home too."

Lottie opened her eyes wide. "Oh! I forgot about Danny!"

"I thought you had," Sofie said rather smugly. "Do not worry, I have told him now. He— Oh! He is coming here. He says you should not wait on your own. But you are not on your own, Lottie, you are with me. He is a silly boy, that one."

Danny thundered up the stairs five minutes later. "Did you get it?" he asked hopefully.

Lottie blinked at him. "Oh . . . the drawing. No, I think she must have it on her."

Danny glared. "Yes, of course the drawing. The whole point of the evening. What's up with

you, Lottie? You look like you've seen a ghost."
He grinned to himself, but then he looked at
Lottie again and his smile faded.

Fred and Peach carefully pulled the photo
out of the rucksack and Danny stared at it.
"That's . . . that's Uncle Tom, isn't it?" he said
at last. "I don't really remember him, but it
doesn't look quite like Dad, so it must be. . .
With *her*. . ."

"Exactly." The cool smoothness of the wall
against her cheek was comforting and Lottie
didn't want to think any more. She was vaguely
aware that Danny was talking to Sofie but it
didn't seem very important. Nothing seemed
very important any more.

"Lottie! Lottie!"

Lottie blinked dazedly and looked up.
Ariadne was sitting on the step next to her, an
arm around her shoulders. Tabitha and
Shadow were on either side of her, their green
eyes glowing like jewels in the darkness

of the stairway.

"Did you see it?" Lottie murmured, gazing up at her. "The photo?"

"Yes, I did. Come on, Lottie, come inside. It's freezing out on these stairs. Your poor mice are practically mauve with cold." She lifted Lottie up and led her into the flat, settling her and Danny at the kitchen table and starting up her enormous coffee machine. "It's all right, Lottie, I'll make hot chocolate for you, but I need coffee to deal with this and so does Sofie."

Lottie nodded. "Oh! The mice! I promised them rose-hip brandy. You don't have any, do you?"

The mice, who had been watching Ariadne's coffee machine with great interest, now stared up at her hopefully.

Ariadne looked doubtful. "No. . . I have some cowslip wine that one of my aunts gave me. It's at the back of a cupboard somewhere. . ."

"That would do," Fred said swiftly.

Ariadne didn't have any thimbles either, but the mice assured her politely that they would slum it and drink out of egg cups, no problem at all.

The hot chocolate was very sweet and comforting and Lottie felt much better after only a couple of sips. "What did you put in this?" she asked Ariadne suspiciously, watching the pink steam rising from her cup and coiling in delicate patterns towards the ceiling.

"Ask me no questions and I'll tell you no lies," Shadow growled. He was very protective of his mistress. "A saying you'd do well to remember, Lottie."

"Ssshhh, Shadow." Ariadne stroked his head. "Lottie, don't worry, it's just essence of roses. It's an old recipe, that's all. No magic. Well, only a little. It's only to make you feel a bit better."

"I don't want to feel better!" Lottie snapped,

banging her mug down on the table. "I want everybody to stop pretending and tell me what's really going on. I've seen the proof. You can't lie to me any more."

"Did Uncle Tom really go out with that . . . that. . ." Danny tailed off.

"Pandora?" Ariadne sighed. "Yes, he did. For five years. They were childhood sweethearts. Everyone thought they'd be together for ever."

"They really loved each other?" Lottie asked in a small voice.

Ariadne nodded, looking at Lottie sympathetically. "I know you don't want to hear it, Lottie, but yes. They were so close. That's why it hit them so hard when it went wrong."

"What happened?" Lottie demanded. "Did you know them all then?"

"Ariadne was my mum's best friend," Danny explained.

Ariadne shrugged. "Pandora's magic happened. The mind-twisting stuff she does.

Tom closed his eyes to it for a long while. He couldn't admit to himself what she was doing, you see. Jack spoke to him about it eventually, pointed out that she was going too far. Tom went mad. He was furious. He hit Jack, knocked him out, and that's when he realized, when he saw his brother stretched out on the floor. She'd been doing it to him too. She knew Jack didn't like her and she'd been trying to turn Tom against him. She'd forgotten they were brothers. She was an only child herself and I don't think she understood the power of the bond. He ended it after that." Ariadne sighed. "He told her she had to stop, that she was going bad. Of course, the sad thing is, by splitting with her he turned her completely."

"And then he met my mum?" Lottie asked.

"A few months after, yes." Ariadne smiled. "They were so different, Isobel and Pandora. To be honest, Lottie, I think that was one of the things that your dad liked about her straight away."

Lottie shook her head. "Ever since I got here, I couldn't think how he could marry someone who didn't understand magic. I suppose that was why. . ."

"Yes, but he didn't just go out and find the first non-magical girl he could, Lottie. He swore for a while that he'd never let himself love anyone, in case they did that to him again." Ariadne took a sip of coffee and grinned, remembering. "He resisted your mum as hard as he could, but she bewitched him even more than Pandora had, without any magic at all."

"Was Pandora still around?" Danny asked. "I can't see her giving up easily, somehow."

"She couldn't believe he'd split up with her." Ariadne shivered. "She wasn't quite as strong then as she is now, but she was powerful enough to be a dangerous enemy. Especially for someone like Isobel, who had no idea what she really was. She kept on trying too, over the years. Even though she'd moved away from

Netherbridge, every so often Tom would get a letter from her, or he'd go around looking ill for a few days, and you'd know she'd had another go at his mind. But he loved your mum so much, Pandora could never twist his thoughts away from her."

Lottie was amazed by the sudden surge of protective love she felt for her mother at the thought of Pandora attacking her. "Did she hurt my mum?" she demanded.

"She tried. And she tried to tell your mum about the magic too. Isobel thought she was mad." Ariadne sighed. "It would have been funny if it weren't so sad. The odd thing is, I'm sure Pandora could have killed Isobel if she'd tried hard enough. But that didn't seem to be what she wanted. I suppose killing her wouldn't have got Tom back. And Pandora was more subtle than that. I do wonder. . ." she trailed off.

"What?" Lottie glared at her. "Come on, Ariadne, what were you going to say?"

Ariadne looked at her thoughtfully. "I

wonder whether Isobel would have accepted the idea of magic one day if it hadn't been for Pandora. Pandora closed her mind to it entirely. I think Tom always hoped that she would understand eventually, especially when you were born. But it never happened. I mean, you saw what your mum was like when she came here again – she had no idea. She didn't remember that she'd met me before, even. It's as though that time is gone for her."

Lottie blinked as she imagined the life she would have had if her mother had understood about magic. She wouldn't have taken Lottie away from here, surely, if she'd known? She wouldn't have felt so alone in Netherbridge that she had to leave. And Lottie's dad might not have wanted to go off on his unbelievably stupid search for unicorns if her mum had understood him more. Lottie dug her fingernails into her palms to stop herself howling as she finally understood what Pandora had taken away from her.

Then she gasped. Unbelievably stupid. Far too stupid to believe. . .

"What is it?" Ariadne asked her anxiously. "Lottie, sweetheart, what's wrong?"

"The unicorns! My dad, when he disappeared, Uncle Jack said he went to search for unicorns in the rainforest somewhere and he never came back."

"Unicorns! That's a fairy story!" Danny laughed, and then looked immediately sorry as he saw Lottie's face.

"I know! It was mad. My dad was mad enough about them to leave me and my mum even when she didn't want him to go." She looked round at them all. "Don't you see? It wasn't real! Pandora got to him at last. She planted it in his mind, I know she did. She stopped trying to get my dad back, but she couldn't stand for my mother to win, so she killed him. She didn't kill my mum, she killed him instead. So no one could have him if she couldn't. She sent him out there to die."

Chapter 8

"Lottie, you can't be sure of that," Ariadne began soothingly.

"Don't you think it's true?" Lottie demanded, fixing her eyes on Ariadne's.

Ariadne faltered. "I— I don't know, Lottie. It did seem a strange thing for him to do. I remember thinking so at the time, when your aunt told me. But then, I remember he always was a bit odd about unicorns. He wanted to believe in them so much. They were one of his pet dreams."

"Pandora would have known that too," Lottie said quietly. "She would have known just how to trick him. I know I can't prove it. But I'm sure, really, really sure. As soon as I thought of it, I could feel it was true." She was silent for a moment, then she looked up at

Ariadne and Danny again. "She didn't know about me, did she? She bit her lip so hard she drew blood when Uncle Jack told her I wasn't his daughter. Did she never know that my mum and dad had a baby?"

"She'd gone away, hadn't she?" Danny put in. "Before you were born. She might not have found out."

"She tried to attack me in that dream the same night she found out who I was," Lottie remembered. "She asked if I wanted to be her apprentice instead of yours, Ariadne. She wants my dad's child under her control."

"Or dead," Danny added. Everyone glared at him and he shrugged. "Sorry, Lottie, but I reckon it's true. She's mad."

Lottie drank the last of her chocolate and stood up, reaching for her coat.

"Are you going home?" Ariadne asked, slightly surprised.

Lottie wrapped her scarf round her neck thoughtfully. "No. I'm going back to Pandora's shop. I want to talk to her."

"*What?*" Ariadne, Sofie and Danny all spoke at once.

"Lottie, you can't! You don't know what could happen." Ariadne got up and took her hands. "And in her shop, on her territory, she'll have the advantage. She'll break down your defences."

"No, she won't. Or maybe she will, I don't know. I'm not just going to go home and pretend this didn't happen. She killed my dad, Ariadne!" Lottie's voice shook.

"You can't go after her in this state," Shadow pronounced.

"She can't do it at all!" Ariadne told him angrily.

"She has to," Sofie whispered. "Lottie is right. But not tonight. Wait, Lottie, till tomorrow."

"It won't be any easier to fight her tomorrow." Ariadne gave Lottie a little shake. "This is madness."

Lottie laughed, trembling. "Well, she's mad too, isn't she? We'll be even. I have to, like Sofie said. I can't not. You told me once that there was no point having magic if I wouldn't use it. This is when I need to use it, Ariadne. Now or never."

Ariadne looked at her. "Maybe you are ready," she said quietly. "Do you want me to come with you?"

Lottie shook her head. She did, actually, but she had a strong feeling that she had to do this on her own. She'd wondered about asking Danny to come, but she didn't want her big cousin along to look after her. Much. She had a sudden thought and looked anxiously at Sofie.

"Of course I am coming," the little dog told her irritably. "But we are definitely waiting until tomorrow. Halloween is Pandora's time, not ours. She is the one who needs the dark. The night powers."

Lottie smiled at her. "Mmm. We're definitely sunshine witches."

Ariadne put her hands on Lottie's shoulders. "I think Sofie is right that you shouldn't go now. You're too upset, too angry. But remember the anger, and use it, Lottie! Control it, make sure it doesn't control you. Don't let it die down." Her voice was quiet and sad as she added, "You're very strong, Lottie, stronger than you realize. But you're going to need everything you've got against Pandora."

Lottie shivered. It was hard to believe that she was about to confront a powerful – and mad – enchantress, with only a small dog for company.

The next morning, Lottie woke up with the same strange anxious feeling that she sometimes got before a big test at school. At first she couldn't remember why, but then she saw Sofie lying on the duvet next to her with her paws in the air and snoring gently. All at once it flooded back. She was a witch who'd inherited her magic from her father. He'd been killed by another witch, an evil one, and today Lottie was going to fight back for him — or perhaps be killed too. She didn't know yet.

The temptation to turn over and go back to sleep was very strong.

"Sofie," she whispered.

Sofie opened one eye sleepily and then shook her ears. "I think this is a good day for chocolate before breakfast, Lottie, hmmm?"

Lottie grinned. "You're probably right. In fact maybe we ought to have some chocolate and then get dressed quickly and grab a couple of slices of toast. Uncle Jack doesn't usually open the shop on Sundays, so he'll be having a lie-in, and I shouldn't think Danny's planning to get up at all. I don't want Uncle Jack asking us questions about where we're going."

Sofie shook her head. "No. You are not a very good liar, Lottie. It is something we should work on. I do not think your uncle will be down for a while though. He was probably out on Netherbridge Hill last night, looking for that unicorn."

Lottie shuddered. "I hope he didn't meet Pandora."

They crept downstairs to make toast and then sat looking at each other over the crumbs.

"Shall we go then?" Lottie said, taking a deep breath, which was difficult. Her chest seemed to have gone all tight.

"Mmmm." Sofie licked the last drops of coffee out of her pink china bowl. "*Allons-y*. I mean, let us go, Lottie. You must learn more French," she said sternly in response to Lottie's blank look.

"I promise I will," Lottie told her. It felt good to talk about what was going to happen after today. It meant that there was actually going to *be* an after today. Lottie wondered suddenly if she ought to have rung her mum. But then what would she have said? *Hi Mum. Just thought I'd call in case I never see you again*?

It felt strange to walk down the street with only Sofie in her arms. Lottie felt as though she ought to be more prepared, even have some sort of weapon.

Pandora wasn't in the shop but the door opened when Lottie pushed it, so she and Sofie simply walked inside. The silvery bell tinkled, its notes ringing horribly in Lottie's ears.

Sofie shook her head irritably. "That bell is . . . is *wrong*!" she pronounced.

"It's a spell bell!" Lottie said, giggling foolishly.

Sofie gave her a sharp look but Lottie stopped laughing. "It's all right, I'm just nervous. It wasn't the spell."

Another door at the back of the shop opened and Pandora walked in, a wary look on her face. The door obviously led to the garden and she was carrying a bunch of herbs. The odd, bitter smell reached as far as Lottie was standing and Sofie sneezed.

Pandora smiled thinly. She didn't seem too surprised to see them. The salukis slid through the door past Pandora and let out a low, throbbing growl, hardly more than a breath.

"Be careful, Sofie!" Lottie warned.

"They do not scare me!" Sofie hissed.

"I know, that's why I'm worried!" Lottie put a firm hand on Sofie's collar.

The little dog is very brave, Lottie. A silky voice was filling her head, and it made her shudder. *But you aren't quite so brave, are you?*

"I'm here, aren't I?" Lottie snapped back, out loud. She didn't want Pandora in her head.

"But you're shaking, Lottie, and your heart is beating so fast," Pandora purred. "Yes, I can feel it, you know. I'm inside you already and I could put my hand round your heart and squeeze it lifeless in a second."

"That's not true!" Lottie tried to sound confident, but all at once she was sure she could feel Pandora's fingers creeping through her veins and Pandora's breath in her throat. She was choking!

Lottie, stop! If you believe it, then it is so! Listen, Lottie, she is lying to you!

Sofie's cross little voice broke the spell and Lottie's head snapped up. She shook her dark curls out of her eyes angrily and saw Pandora wince.

Now! Now! Sofie snapped, and together their thoughts surged towards Pandora in her moment of weakness.

Her mind was a seething mass of bitterness. *So like her father. Same eyes, those same black curls. He betrayed me, and he paid for it. She'll pay too, the worthless little brat! But she's strong. I'll have her power. Make her mine. Use her. Then perhaps I'll kill her – Ah!*

She'd discovered Lottie and Sofie, and in a furious burst of anger, she flung them out of her mind.

Pandora was so strong it was like being struck by lightning. A burst of white light exploded behind Lottie's eyes and it was followed by cold blackness. Lottie tried to open her eyes and found that they were already open. The darkness was still there. She knew

173

she was Lottie – or was she? She thought she was. But she knew nothing else. Not where, or who, or how.

Perhaps she should close her eyes again and go to sleep? There seemed nothing else to do, after all. . . And if she closed her eyes, that horrible blackness might go away. . .

"Lottie!" It was a scream and it shattered the blackness into a thousand tiny diamonds. Lottie was lying on the floor of the shop, curled up into a ball, with Sofie staring at her.

Lottie blinked. "Why's there a hamster on your head?"

The hamster leaned forward. "It's me, Lottie, old thing. Giles. I, er, had to wake Sofie up. She woke you. Very powerful scream she has there."

"He bit me," Sofie said pathetically, holding up one paw.

"Did you follow us?" Lottie asked. She was starting to feel a bit more like herself.

"No, I was in your pocket the whole time. Felt you needed some back-up. The reserves, you know. Not good to show the entire force to the enemy."

Lottie made a small noise that sounded like *Eep!* "Pandora! I'd forgotten her, where is she?"

"I think it wore her out when she threw that light at us," Sofie explained. "But we have not got long, I think." She nodded over at the counter. Pandora was sitting leaning against it with the salukis nosing at her face. Even as Sofie spoke, she stared over at Lottie and stood up, pushing the dogs away. They whined softly and she snarled at them to be quiet.

"You can tell what someone's like from the way they treat animals." It was something Uncle Jack often said. Lottie realized it was true as she said it.

"So noble. Your father's daughter, Lottie. Tom was noble too. That's why he was so obsessed with those stupid unicorns. He thought they were the noblest creatures ever to have lived."

"It *was* you who sent him after them, then." Lottie clenched her fists.

"Of course. You know it was. I heard some ridiculous rumour and I made sure it got to Tom. I knew how he'd take it. Then I arranged for him to encounter some . . . friends of mine while he was out there."

"You killed him!"

"Oh yes, Lottie. I made sure he died alone. And I'd do it again, in a heartbeat. . ." Pandora's purring laugh filled the shop and filled Lottie's mind in a swirl of anger and hate. She dimly heard Sofie screaming again and Giles crying, "Lottie, no! Don't let her do this to you!" But Lottie wasn't there any more. She was lost in a fire of fury and revenge.

I've won! I've won! A triumphant whisper filled Lottie's ears and she turned, twisting, her eyes burning. Where was she? Pandora had trapped her again and she couldn't feel

Sofie, or Giles.

I got too caught up in my anger, Lottie told herself, miserably. *She's made me like her. It's what Ariadne told me not to do. That's why she wouldn't let me come here last night. Oh, I've been so stupid!*

Pandora's whisper was now a painful shrilling cry in Lottie's mind. *You certainly have. And now I have you, I can use you, Lottie darling. Your mother, your irritatingly disapproving uncle. Your cousin. I'll get to them all through you. Just like I used your little friend.*

Lottie shook her head desperately. *No! I won't let you! Oh, help, someone help me!*

There isn't anyone, Pandora snapped. But Lottie detected just a thread of unease in her voice and she called again. *Help, help me, please!*

All at once the redness seemed to cool and another voice was there.

You only had to call, Lottie. I'll always come. And the white unicorn was standing at her shoulder, facing Pandora with her, and Sofie had leaped into her arms and was licking her cheek lovingly.

You! Pandora screamed and Lottie gasped.

She knew who the unicorn was.

It was her father.

"Lottie! Lottie, wake up!"

Lottie gasped and jumped awake.

"Oh, thank goodness, I thought you were dead!" Ruby hugged her. "Are you all right?"

Lottie looked round. She was still in the shop but there was no sign of Pandora or the unicorn. Sofie was curled in her lap, looking as confused as she felt, and Giles was standing on the shop counter staring round anxiously.

"No sign!" he reported. "She got away, I think."

"Lottie. . ." Ruby looked round the shop, her eyes bewildered. "Lottie, was the woman who ran this place a *witch*?"

"Of course she was!" Sofie snapped. "And you have a lot of apologizing to do. You have been most unpleasant. You deserved to be bitten!"

"Sofie, that isn't fair," Lottie protested. "Ruby was under a spell."

"Was I?" Ruby muttered. "That explains things. I can't remember anything about the last week. Just these odd flashes here and there. Then I found myself standing outside this shop, and then I saw you lying on the floor."

"Ruby, I met my dad!" Lottie's eyes were shining with excitement. "Only in a sort of dream and he was a unicorn, but it was him. He's not dead." She looked uncertainly at Sofie. "At least, I don't think he can be."

Sofie shrugged. "I do not know. He felt real. But it could have been a memory, perhaps?"

"Your dad's a *horse*?" Ruby asked, staring at her worriedly.

Lottie grinned at her tiredly. "Don't look at me like that. Let's go home. I promise I will explain, I just can't work it all out myself right now. Please come back with me?"

Ruby nodded, still looking dazed. She pulled Lottie up and Lottie staggered to her feet, clutching Sofie, and Giles jumped on to her shoulder. "Lottie, manners!" he whispered as they walked out into the sunshine. "Introduce this young lady!"

"Oh, yes. Ruby, this is Giles. He's a hamster. Giles, this is Ruby." Lottie put an arm round her. "She's my best friend."

Although Sofie drinks enormous amounts of coffee and gobbles chocolate, this is only because she is a magical dog. Chocolate can be very dangerous for dogs, so please don't feed your dogs chocolate, or anything that isn't their normal food. Even if you suspect they're magical inside!

—HW

Ready for more

adventures with Lottie?

Here's a sneak peek of

Animal Magic

Rabbitmagic

HOLLY WEBB

Chapter 1

Lottie walked slowly up the street, her dachshund Sofie held tightly in her arms, and Giles the hamster perched on her shoulder. Her best friend, Ruby, walked next to her, close enough that Lottie could hear her breathing. It was early on Sunday morning.

Lottie laughed to herself, hugging Sofie closer.

"What is it?" Ruby asked. She looked pale, but she seemed fine otherwise, Lottie thought, looking at her carefully. The spell that had been put on Ruby was definitely gone.

"Oh, I was just thinking. . . When Mum sent me to live here, I had no idea what it would be like. I was just angry that she'd dumped me on Uncle Jack. If you'd told me – what, four months ago? – that I'd be living in a shop full of magical animals, I'd never have believed you." Lottie shook her head wonderingly.

"Do you – do you wish you hadn't?" Ruby asked her slowly.

Lottie looked up sharply. "Of course not!" She felt Sofie's tense muscles shift with relief. Sofie was Lottie's familiar, her spell-companion, and they were learning magic together. But Sofie was never quite sure how much Lottie loved her, whether she would suddenly decide to go back to her mother, and leave Sofie behind here in Netherbridge. "How could I?" Lottie asked. "There's Sofie, and you, and Uncle Jack and Danny. And all the other animals in the shop. I wouldn't ever want to go back to how I was before. When animals didn't talk, and magic was just in fairy tales." Lottie shivered a little, rubbing her cheek against Sofie's velvet ear, and Sofie licked her lovingly. "It would be better if it was just the good bits of fairy tales, though. I'm not so keen on the evil enchantresses like Pandora. If you'd said we'd be going out on a Sunday morning to fight one of those, I'd have thought you were as mad as Pandora is."

Lottie and Ruby looked at each other and grinned. Lottie had just survived doing the most stupid thing she'd ever done. She still didn't know how. She and Sofie had walked willingly into a fight with a crazed witch. They'd had to. Pandora had had Ruby under a spell, stitched into an enchanted drawing, and it was the only way to save her. Lottie wasn't quite sure how they'd got out alive, let alone how they still had control over their own minds. She shook her head slowly. Everything still seemed to work.

They pushed open the door of Grace's Pet Shop, making the bell jangle cheerfully, and Uncle Jack looked round the door that led on to the kitchen, holding a doorstep of peanut butter toast. "Oh, it's you lot. What are you doing up so early on a Sunday, girls? Want some toast?"

"Can we take it upstairs?" Lottie asked. She was going to have to explain where she'd been to Uncle Jack sometime soon, she knew, but she wanted to talk over everything that had happened with the others first.

Uncle Jack sliced huge wodges of bread and slid them under the grill, and a couple of minutes later Lottie carried a teetering pile of hot buttered toast up the stairs to her room.

"You might bang on Danny's door and ask if he wants breakfast," Uncle Jack called after them. "On second thought, don't worry, he can make his own; he hasn't set fire to the kitchen for a few months now. If anyone needs me I'll be in the workroom. I've got a big order for Fido's Fang Polish." This was Uncle Jack's own brand of dog toothpaste. It was very popular with dogs, because it was liver flavoured, though he carefully didn't specify liver of what, in case it upset people.

Ruby giggled as they shut the bedroom door and curled up on Lottie's bed with the toast.

"Your uncle is so funny. Has your cousin really set the kitchen on fire?"

Lottie let Sofie answer – she'd lived with the family a lot longer than Lottie had. Danny hadn't had any major accidents since Lottie had lived there.

Sofie nodded, the toast crusts sticking out of the corners of her mouth. "Mmmpf. Twice. And when he was four, he flooded it as well. He was trying to make his mother a cup of tea in bed. He put the tea bags in the kettle, and then he left the tap running when he took the tea upstairs."

Lottie smiled sadly. Danny's mum had died when he was seven. Lottie missed her own mum, who was living in Paris at the moment, but at least she got to see her every so often, and they could talk on the phone and send emails. She was there in the background. Lottie couldn't imagine not having a mum at all, like Danny. At least Danny had his dad. Lottie couldn't even remember hers. He'd disappeared when she was two, and had never been heard from again. She couldn't help envying that Danny had his father – well, sometimes. Uncle Jack was great, but he was so scatty! He wasn't much help if you had an emergency geography project and needed a papier-mâché volcano yesterday. Lottie had a feeling that Danny's mum was the kind of person who'd always made sure geography projects got done a fortnight in advance. Which partly explained why Danny and Uncle Jack were now both unbelievably disorganized.

Funnily enough, Uncle Jack was very organized when it came to the shop. He never forgot to feed the animals, or clean out their cages. Although of course it helped that they would complain very loudly if he did.

Lottie jumped as her bedroom door opened. Danny lurched round the door, dressed in tracksuit bottoms and an enormous sweater.

"You've got toast," he told Lottie accusingly. "I could smell it. Gimme some. Pleeease," he added, as Lottie pulled the toast closer to her. "I'm starved. Hi Ruby." He blinked. "What time is it?"

"About nine," Lottie said. "OK, you can have one piece. And you and Sep have to share!" she added, seeing Danny's black rat appear from his sweater pocket, his whiskers quivering in anticipation of toast.

"Is there peanut butter?" Septimus enquired, leaning over to admire the toast.

"No," Lottie told him firmly. Septimus was incredibly lazy, and very persuasive, much like Danny. She knew he was quite capable of sweet-talking her into going downstairs to get it for him, probably accompanied by another five or so pieces of toast.

"What were you doing up this early?" Danny asked, dropping crumbs all over Lottie's duvet.

"Early!" Giles the hamster tutted. "Best part of the day is before dawn." He nibbled his toast crust delicately for such a chubby creature, filling his enormous pouches.

Septimus eyed him with dislike. "Hamsters, dear chap, are nocturnal. You sleep all day, when we are hard at work."

Lottie half-choked. Septimus went to school with Danny in his blazer pocket, but neither of them did any work at all.

"Lottie fought Pandora," Sofie told him proudly, as she slyly sneaked another slice of toast.

"What?" Danny yelled, almost dropping his second piece, which he was hoping Lottie hadn't noticed. "Are you crazy? You went and did it on your own?"

"You knew I was going to!" Lottie protested. "You were there when I was talking to Ariadne about it."

Ariadne was Uncle Jack's girlfriend, and a witch. She was helping Lottie find and develop her own magic. Lottie had ended up at Ariadne's flat the previous night. After she'd found a photograph of Pandora with her father, she'd needed answers. Uncle Jack wouldn't tell her what had happened to his brother all that time ago, but Lottie had been sure Ariadne would see that she had to know. She couldn't bear being kept in the dark any longer. Did Pandora have something to do with her dad's disappearance? It had been really weird for Lottie, finding out about her magical family, especially without her dad there. She'd inherited the magic from him, but she didn't have him to teach her – she'd had no idea at all what had happened to him, until odd things had started to happen recently. Ariadne knew and understood all of this, so Lottie trusted her to tell the truth.

"I wasn't going to let you go off, not without someone there for backup," Danny muttered. "I can't believe you just went off and faced her, while I was asleep!"

Lottie wasn't sure if he was cross because she'd done something dangerous, or because he'd missed an adventure, or both.

"She had me!" Sofie said in an indignant growl.

"Hamsters are always proud to be of service," Giles put in.

"And you had me too. . ." Ruby added. "Well, I suppose I wasn't much use." She smiled at Lottie, then she shook her head. "I still can't believe Pandora put me under a spell. It's just – horrible."

"*You* were horrible," Sofie told her sternly. "You were very unkind to Lottie."

Ruby looked hurt. "I'm sorry," she muttered.

"Sofie! It wasn't Ruby's fault!" Lottie put an arm round Ruby's shoulders. "I should be saying sorry to you. None of this would have happened if you hadn't been my friend. Pandora was using you to get to me, that's the kind of person she is."

"Stop wittering," Danny demanded. "What happened? I mean, you must have won. Unless you're bewitched now – are you?" He stared suspiciously at Lottie, glaring into her eyes, until she grabbed the last bit of toast and shoved into his mouth.

"Shut up, of course we're not." Lottie looked down at her hands. "I don't honestly know what happened. How it ended, I mean, how we survived," she admitted. "It was really weird. . . I . . . I think I saw my dad." She looked up at Danny almost shyly, not sure what he was going to think of her. She wasn't prepared for the expression of pure hurt that flashed across his face, but the moment she saw it she would have given anything to take back what she'd just said.

Danny's voice was slightly flat, but that was the only sign that she'd upset him. "I don't get it. A ghost, you mean?"

"No!" Lottie wasn't sure how she knew that her dad was alive after all, but she did. She didn't look at Danny. There wasn't an easy way to tell him. Having lost her dad, like he'd lost his mum, had always bonded them together, even though they never spoke about it. "No. I think he was real. I'm sure he was." She sighed. "But he was a unicorn." She waited for Danny to snigger. Even Ruby had thought she was being a bit mad when she'd told her.

Danny leaned back against the wall. "OK. Tell me the whole thing."

Lottie settled her shoulders against the wall next to him and closed her eyes, remembering. "It was awful. Pandora got inside me somehow, and said she could squeeze my heart so it would stop beating—"

"She couldn't do that!" Danny scoffed. Then he looked doubtfully at Sofie. "Could she?"

Sofie shrugged. "I do not know. Perhaps. But she was not trying to. She was just scaring Lottie. And it worked."

"She was scary! I can't help it!" Lottie complained. "She terrifies me. Anyway, Sofie told me she was just pretending, and I snapped out of it, and that made Pandora so cross that she left herself open, and we slipped into her mind."

"Wow!" Ruby gasped. "You didn't tell me that! How did you do it? What was it like?"

Sitting either side of her on the bed, the other two felt Lottie shake slightly. It frightened her even to remember. "Awful. She was so cold, like there wasn't much person left inside her any more. She was frozen."

"We did not stay for long." Sofie laughed, a grim, grunting little chuckle.

"She threw us out, and that was – it was – there was nothing. Only black. I didn't know who I was, even." Lottie smiled gratefully at Giles, who was leaning against her pillow with his paws folded happily across his stomach. "Giles saved us."

"My paw is still not better," Sofie mourned. "I do not think you needed to bite me quite so hard."

"Sofie, dear old thing, you were both unconscious," Giles explained. "I had no choice. I am not by nature a creature of violence –" everyone spluttered slightly, as Giles was a particularly warlike hamster – "but it was necessary in this instance. You woke up, and you woke Lottie up."

"Then what happened?" Ruby asked anxiously.

Lottie frowned, and bit her lip. "Then – I did something stupid. I let her make me angry. She told me she had killed my dad – or she'd sent him to die, anyway. But as soon as I got angry, I was trapped. There was a fire. I mean, I know it was all in my head, but it seemed so real!"

Danny shook his head. "Elementary mistake," he said, in a disapproving, older-brotherly voice.

Lottie glared at him. "I'd like to see you taking it and not getting angry, Mr I'm-going-to-glamour-myself-until-I-fall-off-a-skateboard!"

Danny shrugged, but didn't argue. When he'd started secondary school, he'd tried to use his own magic to make himself popular, but it hadn't worked very well. "Go on then. When did the unicorn come in?"

"About then," Lottie said slowly, remembering. "I called for help. Like I did that time before, when Pandora was in my mind when I was asleep. The unicorn came that time too, and chased her away."

Danny nodded. "Yeah, Dad said about that. He thought you just imagined it. You didn't say it was your dad then, though, did you?"

Lottie blinked. "No. . . I didn't realize. Come on, Danny, it was a unicorn! And everyone's always told me my dad was dead! What was I supposed to think?"

"So how do you know it was him this time? Did he say so?" Danny's face was painfully eager.

"No. He just said he'd always come if I called him, I only had to ask. But Pandora recognized him; she yelled, 'You!' She screamed it out, like it was being . . . torn out of her heart. . ."

Lottie took a deep breath. "It was then I realized who he was. Pandora sort of stepped back, and she was staring at us both. I don't think she could have hurt us; it was like she was in shock. Then I don't know what happened, but the unicorn was gone, and so was Pandora."

"But how? How could you tell it was him?" Danny demanded again, and Lottie looked at him helplessly.

"I'm so sorry," she whispered. "I just could."

"I don't understand," Ruby murmured. "I mean, I don't understand any of it really, but what I don't get is why your dad turning up shocked Pandora so much. She'd tried to kill him, I guess. Was that it? She thought he was dead, and he wasn't?"

Lottie laughed, but it wasn't a happy laugh. She sounded bitter. "Sorry, Ruby, I forgot you didn't hear about that. I found it all out while you were under that spell. Pandora was my dad's old girlfriend."

Join Lottie in all of her

adventures.

Holly has always loved animals. As a child, she had two dogs, a cat, and at one point, nine gerbils (an accident). Holly's other love is books. Holly now lives in Reading with her husband, three sons and a very spoilt cat.